Books by Ouida Sebestyen

Words by Heart
Far from Home
IOU's

# ❧IOU's❧

# ❧IOU's❧

## by

## Ouida Sebestyen

*An Atlantic Monthly Press Book*
**Little, Brown and Company**
**BOSTON      TORONTO**

J
S

FIRST EDITION

*Library of Congress Cataloging in Publication Data*

Sebestyen, Ouida.
   IOU's.

   "An Atlantic Monthly Press book."
   Summary: Thirteen-year-old Stowe Garrett is
caught between the loyalty and love he feels for
his mother and a yearning to break free and experi-
ment with life.
   I. Title. II. Title: I.O.U.'s.
PZ7.S444Iac      [Fic]        82–124
ISBN 0–316–77933–4          AACR2

ATLANTIC-LITTLE, BROWN BOOKS
ARE PUBLISHED BY
LITTLE, BROWN AND COMPANY
IN ASSOCIATION WITH
THE ATLANTIC MONTHLY PRESS

BP

BOOK DESIGNED BY S.M. SHERMAN

*Published simultaneously in Canada
by Little, Brown & Company (Canada) Limited*

PRINTED IN THE UNITED STATES OF AMERICA

To the S and S Company
and all the others who shared
their thirteenth summer

# •IOU's•

# ⇒ One ⇐

S towe Garrett was halfway out the front door when the phone rang. His mother was already on the sidewalk, with Tyler hanging from one hand and a diaper bag from the other. "Talk fast," she called. "Tell him we're running late." Fat drops of rain began to fall around her.

It used to amaze him that Annie knew who was on the phone before he answered, until he realized that some natural law caused his friend Brownie to call just as they were rushing off somewhere. He snatched up the receiver and said briskly, "We're running late."

Brownie's voice, as inevitable as gravity, said, "Where to?"

Stowe glanced out at Annie. "Well, we've got to take Tyler over to his house because his dad's transmission fell out and he couldn't come get him. And we still haven't got our groceries because Yetta's mother was late picking her up and that's making us late."

Lightning crackled in his ear. He swung the receiver farther away. Through the doorway he could see Tyler's little hands grabbing for the leg of Annie's faded jeans.

She bent and gathered him up just before the thunder got him.

"I called, but you were doing papers," Brownie said. "What was your mom so mad about — had she just grounded you for something?"

"Mad?" The word darkened him like a cloud. Then he remembered. "She wasn't mad. Just upset. She got this letter that her dad's sick in the hospital with a heart attack."

"Oh." There was a pause while Brownie took a bite of something. "How come she knew about it if they don't speak to each other?"

Stowe glanced out. Brownie always remembered the very thing he wished he hadn't revealed. "Well, *he* doesn't want to have anything to do with us, but my great-aunt Fritzi wrote."

"So if they hate each other like that, why's she so upset?"

"It's not hate, exactly." It was hard to explain, even to himself, why Annie should be so upset about somebody who hadn't spoken to her all these years. He watched her hurry back up on the porch, holding Tyler in her arms and laughing so he'd think thunderstorms were fun. In a lower voice he said, "But that's what upsets her, I guess. The not-getting-along part. Anyway, right on top of that, Sir Landlard came waddling out and raised our rent again."

"Sounds like he's all heart, too," Brownie said.

"Yeah. Just three hundred pounds of heart."

Brownie laughed. "So are you coming over? It's a neat movie on TV tonight about this guy that grinds people up

2

in his garbage disposal." He waited in one of the silences
Stowe dreaded. "Might give you some great ideas how to
get rid of a landlord."

"Yeah." Stowe tried to make his hurried breath sound
like a laugh. "I wanted to. But I can't tonight."

"Why? What's after groceries?"

He wished he could blurt things out the way Brownie
did. Like, Hey, just butt out of my business, okay? But he
said, "Oh, other stuff."

"Jeez," Brownie said tiredly. "You've got to go help at
another nursery."

Rain began to pour like a toilet overflowing. Annie
backed into the house, breaking the stranglehold Tyler
had taken on her neck when the thunder clapped again.
She held up her wristwatch, looking anxious.

"I don't *have* to go help," Stowe said in automatic
defense. He struggled in a silence of his own. It was true
he didn't have to go. Or want to, either. But all the same
he was going. He always seemed to be explaining something complicated about himself to Brownie.

"Well, if you don't have to, don't. Jeez, tell her it's *her*
job and you're not going."

Stowe glanced at his mother. "Oh, sure," he agreed
cautiously. That would be easier to say, it seemed to him,
if the money Annie made didn't go to buy his food and
clothes. He took a step toward her to show he was
coming. "Listen, we've got to hurry."

"So hurry," Brownie said with a chopped laugh. "Have
lots of fun sitting babies."

Stowe hung up the receiver. Annie sprinted down off
the porch again with Tyler under her arm like stovewood.

Stowe followed, grabbing up the contest entries he need-ed to mail. He was halfway down the walk when the phone rang again.

"Good grief, what does he want now!" Annie ex-claimed, poking Tyler into the old pickup.

"I don't think it's Brownie this time." Stowe stopped in the rain, held by the strident command of the phone. He turned to Annie. He didn't have a house key of his own the way Brownie did. She sighed and pitched him the whole jangling set. He unlocked the door with stung fingers and ran for the phone.

Always, in his imaginings, when he answered, a rich voice said, Am I speaking to Mr. Garrett? His own voice, plunging to man-of-the-house deepness, always answered, That's correct. Then the voice, practically quivering with respect and excitement, said, I'm with the Thrill-of-a-Lifetime Sweepstakes, Mr. Garrett. Congratulations.

"Hello," he said, puffing a little.

He heard a whisper of distance. Then a middle-aged voice said, "Stowe Garrett?"

His heart flipped. He had won something. "I'm him," he gasped, and sucked in his breath.

"Well, Stowe," the voice said, hesitating. "Uh. Is Annie there?"

He let his breath out. The voice in his fantasy never asked for his mother. "No," he said, realizing that he didn't remember anymore what his father's voice sounded like. He could be talking to his own father and not know it. "She's outside. We were just leaving. Who *is* this?" he asked.

The voice wheezed apologetically. "Well, we're rela-

4

tives, Stowe. Your mother and I are cousins — I'm Harold. Aunt Fritzi's son. I expect you got her letter about your granddad."

"Oh," Stowe breathed. "Yeah. Yes sir. This morning." He tensed, afraid he wouldn't know what to say. "Listen, I'll call my mom."

"Well, actually I guess it's you I want to talk to, Stowe." The voice made breathing noises again. "I don't quite know how to go about it, but here goes."

Stowe clamped his hand over the receiver, rigid with apprehension. Somebody was going to ask him to tell Annie her dad had died.

The voice said, "I've just had a nice long visit with your granddad up at the hospital."

Stowe let his hand slide away in relief. "Is he better?"

"Well, he's out of intensive care. As good as could be expected. But the reason I called, Stowe — well, he got to talking about you."

Involuntarily he glanced out the door at the pickup where Annie waited. "Me?" He felt awkward, suddenly discussing family matters over the phone with a stranger. "You mean, just me?" His fingers traced the phone numbers that other tenants before them had scratched on the wall. "Not my mom?"

"I know there's been trouble a long time," the voice said, breathing earnestly. "I don't take sides on it, because all I know is this side here, and not your mother's. But, yes, he did specify just you." He hesitated. "After I left him I just felt like I ought to tell you what had happened, Stowe. He said things about you that made me think he'd like to see you, really bad."

5

"I guess I don't understand," Stowe said. "Why? He never met me. We don't know each other."

"I know that. And I may be sticking my nose where it don't belong, but I felt like you ought to know he talked to me like that. He wants to see you, Stowe. Now, you and Annie can follow it up or not. I'm not telling you what to do. But if you all talk it over and she wants to put you on the bus or something, well, I'll meet you and you can stay with us and we'll help whatever way we can."

Annie honked the horn. Stowe gave a start and said, "Yeah — well, thanks. A lot. I really appreciate it. So . . ." He searched his mind helplessly for words. "So thank you for telling me."

"Well, I just felt like what if something happened and I hadn't told you. You know? Anyway, you all think about it, and it was good to talk to you, Stowe." There was silence, and a click.

He held the receiver, feeling unreal. The whole thing was as weird as the time some stoned guy called him up and read him a dirty poem. He looked around with the feeling that someone was playing a trick on him. A voice had just told him he ought to hop a bus and rush off, without Annie, to see a man who — until a few minutes ago — had carefully blocked them out of his life.

He said into the dead receiver, "Hey, I'll go when *he* asks me to. Personally! And asks her, too. If he could talk to you like that, he could talk to me. So why didn't he?" He listened to the hum of distance and tension. A longing like cool wind chilled his anger. He cracked the receiver down into its cradle. What things? he wondered. What things did he say about me?

He saw that he was still holding his letters. Slowly he pressed them flat and smoothed the perplexed scowl from his face. He knew he was going to have to think about what had happened. Mull it, by himself, until he knew how he felt about it.

He tucked the letters under his shirt and dashed down the sidewalk. "So whose window did you break with *The Daily Cannonball* this time?" Annie asked, starting the engine as he got in.

He glanced quickly to see if she really had jumped to the conclusion the call had been a complaint from someone on his paper route. He saw nothing but lenient curiosity in her eyes. "I don't break windows anymore," he said. There had been days, at first, when he did. He hesitated, grateful for her mistake but unwilling to lie outright to her, and suddenly gave his voice the pitch he used when he was teasing. "Maybe sometimes I still knock a hole in somebody's screen."

"Oh, Stowe. You didn't." She put Tyler into his lap, and they lurched off. "Always offer to fix it. When it's your fault."

"Oh, sure," he said, looking back at the narrow little house, dingy in the rain. "I always do. When it's my fault." He wished he hadn't heard the phone ringing, either time.

The parking lot at the supermarket was full, but Stowe saw an empty space along the street, and jabbed his finger at it.

"Where-where?" Annie gasped, hitting the brakes. She swerved the old pickup to the curb behind a Cadillac. The loose tailgate made a mimicking *erk-erk*, and Tyler righted himself inside Stowe's arms. Jauntily, like a scene from a funny movie, the rearview mirror outside Annie's window fell off the door.

"All gone," Tyler said, using up half his vocabulary.

They gave each other deadpan Laurel and Hardy stares. "Good grief," Annie snapped. "Seven *more* years' bad luck?"

They turned in unison and peeped through the wobbling rain on their windows to see if anyone had been watching. The street was empty. Out of the silence came a sound Stowe loved. His mother's little whimper slowly grew into a snicker that finally jiggled into a laugh. He leaned back in relief, laughing, too.

"Didn't you promise to replace a certain very necessary screw before this happened?" she asked him.

He lifted his shoulders. At least the brakes still worked and they hadn't started a new seven-year cycle crammed into the trunk of somebody's Cad. "I found a screw. But it was Phillips-head and the Phillips screwdriver dropped behind the washing machine the day the shelf fell down."

Annie groaned and scooted out into the rain. She picked the mirror up. Slivers of glass fell from it as Stowe got Tyler straddled on his hip and came around to her side. "It's all right, Horseless," she murmured, giving a fender the same quick comforting stroke she gave animals and kids. "We get the message. *Never look back*, right?" She pitched the broken mirror into the pickup bed.

They ran for the supermarket. Ordinarily they liked rain too much to hurry through it, especially on a mild

8

August evening, but this time they still had Tyler to deliver, and soon a bunch of impatient choir members would be waiting at the church nursery to dump their little darlings and start practicing their cantata.

Stowe pushed Tyler in the cart as Annie snatched up eggs and oranges and milk for breakfast. Usually she added up prices on a scrap of paper, but he could tell she was trying to do it in her head this time as she rushed from aisle to aisle. He was glad to keep quiet while she counted. He needed to think what he was going to do about that call. He would like to talk to Brownie about it, but it didn't seem right, somehow, to expose Annie's personal problems to anybody.

She asked, "Can't you possibly eat liver without ketchup?"

"It just won't go down," he said. She sighed and grabbed a bottle by its neck. Her lips moved, adding its price to her total. He could tell it was one of those times when she had just a certain amount of money to spend. She always got a pinched look around her mouth that made him feel depressed as he walked beside her.

She ladled whole wheat flour from a bin in the health food section. "Oatmeal or wheat germ for breakfast?"

"Yuck." He sighed. "Oatmeal."

She scooped it into another sack, considered the amount, and put a scoopful back.

"When do we get some real cereal that crunches and sparkles and rots our teeth?" he asked.

She gave him a pretend poke in the eye. "Maybe next time," she promised, using the phrase he had heard all his life. She crooked her finger into Tyler's mouth to see what he was eating. It was a grape. She pushed it back in. "Watch him," she said. "Grapes, yes. Mothballs, no."

"Hey, watermelon," Stowe exclaimed, launching the cart toward it.

Annie craned to see the price. "I thought we'd get one for the picnic. Nearer to next Saturday."

"How about getting one now and another one then?"

She slid her hand uncertainly over the melon's green skin. "How about peaches?" She held out two small ones.

"Big wow," he said flatly, turning away.

She trailed after him, gathering up peanut butter and soap and a bag of potatoes. She looked sad. He stopped and tucked her load into the cart around Tyler. "Peaches are all right," he said.

He got in line to check out while she went back for them. Everybody in town was ahead of him. Annie returned and waited beside him, nervously winding her watch. He wished he didn't get nervous just because she did. A college boy in front of them got out his food stamps to pay for a steak. Annie looked at the window filled with posters and grey rain.

They moved up to the counter. The checker made a tired smile and forced an onion out of Tyler's hand. She dropped it into the sack with the others on the scales.

"Sorry," Annie murmured, and offered Tyler her keys just as his surprised face screwed up to cry.

The ketchup fell over and rolled around and around at the end of the conveyor belt. Stowe righted it and slid it toward the sacker boy. The checker whipped a strip of numbers from the register. "Twenty-one thirty," she said.

Annie reached into her saggy purse. She brought out the wallet Stowe had made in shop. Her mouth twitched. He watched her fingers make shaky little passes over two ten-dollar bills, like a magician trying to make them become two twenties. Slowly she looked up and flashed him a dazed smile. "Got any change?"

He shook his head. "Don't you have —" His mouth stuck on the word. Don't you have *enough?* The people behind her eased their carts forward, watching. He could feel heat surging up through him as if he were a chimney, scorching his face.

"Thought I had it," Annie said to him. She laughed and spread her hands. The man behind her stared. "What can I say?"

"You can make a check, with identification," the checker said, pushing Tyler through in the empty cart.

Stowe watched a glaze come over Annie's lopsided smile. "Well, actually —" She brought out the two tens. "We'll have to leave our groceries in the car for several hours, so I think I'd like to just —" She took the milk out of the sack boy's hands. " — not take this." She hauled the potatoes out of a sack. "Or this."

The checker pressed her mouth thin and recalculated. She handed Annie change. Every muscle in Stowe tensed to ram through all the backed-up carts and let him disappear. Suddenly pennies spilled through Annie's fingers. He knelt, feeling his own hands jerking, and picked them off the floor.

He forced himself to walk beside her as she pushed Tyler and the sacks of groceries past the watching faces. But at the door he bolted ahead, gulping wet air, and

11

scrambled into the pickup. He rested his hot cheek against the glass and watched her coming with the perky smile still frozen on her face.

His letters were lying on the dash. He crawled out again to take them to the mailbox on the corner. "*Win* me something!" he hissed, as they slipped from his fingers into the slot. "Please. Please!"

Annie was waiting. He got in beside her without a word and found places for his big feet between the sacks. She gave him Tyler. "Hey," she said lightly, "people put back groceries all the time. They miscalculate, or forget their checkbooks — "

"No they don't. You do."

"I just thought twenty would do it." She spread her hands hopefully. "Cheer up."

"You had a checkbook." His mouth felt stiff. "You could have made a check."

She watched through the streaked windshield as the Cadillac in front of them pulled out of its parking place. "Nope. It would've bounced. The check for the rent took all I had." The lightness dropped out of her voice. "Stowe. Do you realize what the letter we got this morning means? It means there won't be anything coming tomorrow. Or for who knows how long."

He slid her a glance. His anger slowly melted to an anxiousness that lodged heavily in his stomach.

"Oh, damn," Annie exclaimed, whacking the steering wheel. "I hate these times. It's one thing to run out of money when you know it's at home in another purse, or waiting for you at the bank. But damn when it's not!"

She started off with a jerk. Stowe gazed out over Tyler's

12

head, glumly following the Caddie's taillight far ahead. It didn't help to discover she had been as embarrassed as he had. Actually it was better when she hadn't seemed to care.

The rain thinned as they crossed town. Tyler's dad waited at the covered entrance of his apartment house, peering through the gloom. He waved and ran toward them with his shoulders hunched.

Tyler scrambled up on Stowe's knees and patted the window. Stowe rolled the glass down. Tyler's dad reached in, laughing, and drew Tyler out.

"Hey, cowboy! Did you think I'd forgotten you?" He lifted Tyler high in the rain. Tyler squealed, showing his five teeth. His dad brought him close and they touched foreheads, grinning.

A sudden constricting shyness made Stowe look away. He couldn't remember ever being lifted high like that. But maybe it had happened. He remembered a slap that knocked jellybeans out of his hand, but that might not be fair because there must have been good moments. Loving moments. Or else how could he feel the loss?

"Thanks for bringing him over, Annie," Tyler's dad said in at the window.

"No problem," Annie said. "Sorry about your car."

Tyler's dad smiled unhappily. "I just got the estimate — it's a real budget-buster." A rivulet of rain ran across his glasses. "That brings up something I need to discuss, if you have time." He rubbed Tyler's back with one big hand that almost covered it. "I'm afraid I'm temporarily impoverished."

Annie nodded. "There's a lot of that going around."

13

"I've really got to have this stupid car for my job, and I was wondering if it would be too much to ask . . ."

"Don't worry about it," Annie said.

"I can pay you for sure next week."

"It's all right," Annie said. "But, will your car be fixed by Monday, or —"

"If it's not, I'll get Ty over to you some way."

Annie smiled. She handed the diaper bag to Stowe, who passed it through the window. Tyler's dad waved it as they drove off.

Stowe rolled up the window. Rain had washed the jutting granite and the black forests of the mountain backdrop away. "Why didn't you tell him we needed his stupid money worse than he does?" he asked.

She brought Horseless to a jolting stop at a red light. "It's hard to judge these things, Stowe. He's trying really desperately to keep custody of Tyler — the last thing he needs is problems with the child care. We'll get paid."

Not being able to see the strong silhouette of the mountains left an ache in him. "So what do we eat this week?" he asked.

"Coo, aren't we dramatic?" Annie laughed. She nudged a grocery sack. "Whatever the ravens bring us, child." She stretched her palm toward the steeple of the church up ahead where they were going. "Ask, and ye shall receive."

Just ask? he wondered, thinking of the strange, unknown, unlovable man who had asked for him.

They parked, and ran to the side door of the church. Annie bounded up a flight of stairs into darkness with Stowe behind her, following the slap of her sandals along a windowless hall. She wove through a room full of chairs, not bothering to hunt light switches, and sprinted along a corridor that zigged and zagged until he was completely disoriented. Far ahead, from a lighted door, came a jumble of children's voices.

He braced himself. This was the part he hated, the pretty mothers and the kids and the noise and the diapers and the closed-window church smell. He always tried to get out of it whenever he could, even if it took inviting himself over to someone's house, or promising Annie he'd do the dishes if she'd let him stay at home. He wished he was at Brownie's, watching the guy grind people up. They plunged into the light. Annie made her employee-smile and exclaimed, "Sorry I'm late!"

The mothers faded away. Stowe looked around, catching his breath. Eleven kids already. Two high-school girls were supposed to be there to help, but except for himself and Annie, nobody was over three feet tall.

The smallest was a baby in a canvas seat kind of thing. The older ones, he guessed, were around Yetta's age. She was the nearly-four-year-old they had kept for the last two years. Yetta-canoe and Tyler, too, Annie had said when they took Tyler in. Sometimes they kept other children a day or a week, while their mothers hunted for jobs, or did Vegas with their boy friends, or whatever. Then, as if that weren't enough, Annie took nursery jobs at night.

She opened a cupboard and brought out boxes of toys. Somebody popped three more kids into the room and clapped the door shut. "Obscenity," she whispered to Stowe. It was a word she had taken from a Hemingway book. "This would have been chaos without you." She sat

15

on the floor, holding toys out to entice the shy new kids bunched apprehensively at the door. "Last time, when nobody showed up to help and I didn't have anyone to leave them with, I had to take all ten kids to the bathroom at once."

Stowe smiled back, feeling uncomfortable. He never knew what to do to help. He sat down in a nursery chair so low that his knees nearly hit his chin. Slowly children took over the room like ants, dropping one toy to test another with a senseless kind of intensity, like grown-ups at a sale.

Annie put the baby and his seat behind her, where he would be safe from flying toys and bodies. He seemed to be asleep, his mouth plugged with a pacifier, but suddenly he came unplugged. Annie took him into her lap and soothed his wails.

She looked tired already, Stowe thought. The hard light picked out the grey in her black bunned-up hair. He remembered, back in June when she turned forty, she had sighed and said, "If I'm going to be a cute little white-haired grannylady when I'm eighty, I might as well get started."

"Sure, no use waiting till the last minute," he had agreed, and rushed down to get something for her birthday because she seemed to be having trouble deciding whether to laugh or cry. He didn't think he'd care what had happened to his hair by the time he was forty, but he might feel different in twenty-seven or -eight years. Maybe by that time people would shave their heads. Or wear helmets to keep out pollution. Or he'd be dead, even.

He wished he had a quiet place to sit and gather his thoughts. On the other hand he was glad he didn't, so he could put off thinking as long as possible. He couldn't remember ever deliberately keeping something as important as the phone call from Annie. But it had been to *him*. Whether he shared it or not was his business.

*Think*, Annie was always telling him. He wished he could be like Brownie. Brownie didn't think. He did something. He would either have slammed down the phone in the middle of Cousin Harold's conversation, or he'd be on the bus for Oklahoma now. None of this stupid hesitating. None of this flopping around trying to make the right decision.

"What a day," she said, winding a music box for a little boy who still watched the door where his mother had disappeared. Stowe nodded. Some days, everything fell apart.

The baby's eyes closed. They watched him sleep, bobbing his pacifier occasionally to be sure it was still there. Annie said, "Maybe we should move."

"From our house?" She astounded him. "No! Why? It's home. We can see the mountains."

Some of the kids had jerked stock-still, thinking the No was for them. "Play," Annie said, waving them on.

"What do you mean?" he asked. "Where could we find anything cheaper, except another basement dump like when we first came?" He was never going back to that kind of place, with its halls like tunnels and its backed-up drains. Never. He'd find a cave somewhere first, up in the hogback along the foothills. He'd make them a home in some old miner's cabin with no roof.

"I don't know," she said. "We couldn't. But where's the extra money coming from if Sir Landlard keeps clobbering us every six months?"

The little boy with the music box crawled into her lap beside the baby. "I'm going to make money," Stowe said. He wondered if it would help to say he'd take more lawn-mowing jobs or try harder to get a bigger paper route. Sometimes she only looked sadder when he said things like that. "Really. It's coming." In his mind he commanded the contest entries he had mailed: Win — you've got to.

"And while it's coming?" she asked, smoothing the little boy's stomach in time to the tinky-tink music. "Beans and macaroni? Thrift-store clothes and cringing and skimping, just to see a mountain out your window?"

"Sure," he said. "Even rich people can't buy mountains for their windows." Far away downstairs the choir voices fell silent, revealing a long arc of organ music. He felt silly, trying to cheer her up by making rent money sound easy to come by when it wasn't. He said, "Maybe you could ask — " and stopped, feeling his own stomach tilt anxiously.

"Who?" she asked. "Your father?" She took a long breath. "I think about that. Times like this I'd gladly haul him off to jail for every cent of child support, for alimony, for every pretty promise — "

"But you never have," he said.

"No. Because the next minute I've always realized I don't want his money. I wouldn't take it if he offered." Her jaw got square. "I don't want to ever ask him for help, or be beholden. Does that answer your question?"

18

"But you take money. You take those checks every month, from your dad."

She pressed her mouth into the same tight grimace he had watched her make, each month as long as he could remember, as she slowly slit the envelope that had come.

"Why?" he asked. "What's the difference?"

"I guess the difference is that he doesn't owe it to us."

"But don't you think it's weird? Him sending money to us when he acts like we don't even exist?"

"Yes. I wonder about it, every time — what he's trying to say. Maybe it's some kind of bridge he's trying to keep between us. I don't know how his mind works anymore."

"So maybe it's some kind of dumb way to humiliate us," he said before he could stop. "Reminding us we couldn't make it without him."

"Maybe," she said. She put the baby in his canvas seat. His face wrinkled up, then melted back to sleep. "But even if it is, we need to remember that we *couldn't* make it without him. So I take it. And I pretend that maybe it's sent just because — " He could almost feel her trying to say, "he cares," but she didn't dare.

She looked up into his eyes. He had the terrible feeling that she could see right through them into his mind, where that telephone call was hidden. He leaped out of his chair and rescued a kid who had closed himself up in the cleaning-supply closet.

Carefully he asked, "Did Aunt Fritzi say he had to stay in the hospital long?"

"Not if he starts to improve."

He looked away uncomfortably, trying to imagine what

a heart attack was. Not cavalry galloping through a dust cloud with a bugler sounding Charge. What had attacked? he wondered. What had roared through his grandfather's heart like an army, and made him think of grandsons and dying?

"But she didn't explain, or anything," Annie said. "Just that little short letter."

Stowe went to the window and stared down at the shiny street. Every month, on the fourth day, like a fairy-tale curse, that check had arrived. Tomorrow the August one wouldn't come, Annie had reminded him. Or the ones after that, until his grandfather was well again. Would the thick black scrawl of his signature be different then? he wondered. Even if the printed part still said Lee Earl Albright, Maydell, Oklahoma, the way it always had, would his writing be shaky, changed to match the changed feelings that Cousin Harold had described?

Maybe he owed her the news that her dad was better. Feeling well enough to have Cousin Harold for a visitor just a few hours ago. But how could he tell her that part without telling the rest and adding more pain to the pain she already felt?

A little doll-faced girl went to the door and tried to turn the knob. "Where's my mother?" she asked.

"She'll come soon," Annie promised. "Can you hear her singing?" The children nearby hushed to listen. She said under her breath to Stowe, "The last hour sends everybody up the wall. There's got to be a box of graham crackers in this building. Do you want to poke around, or keep kiddies while I look?"

"You know better where they hide crackers."

The children watched anxiously as she went out, reminded of their mothers' disappearances.

"Me, too," a little boy insisted, scratching at the door.

"You'd get lost out there in all those dark rooms."

"Mommy," the little boy whispered. He went to the diaper-bag shelf and got the grubby scrap of blanket he had brought with him. Sadly he smoothed it against his chest. "Mommy."

"Soon," Stowe promised, wondering what it must be like not to understand that someone would return. A scene flicked across his memory. He was being carried away on a teasing boy's bike. Laughing. Not afraid. Then suddenly he was struggling to jump off, his mouth open in a long quaver of horror. He had realized he was being carried away from Annie. His feet pounded, jolting great gasps of breath out of him. He had to reach her or die. Then, on the sidewalk, far ahead — the red of a sweater. And Annie's arms. Annie's holding-him-forever arms. He gave the little boy an awkward pat. "We can all go home, pretty soon."

Somewhere down the hall, Annie screamed.

Stowe hung a second, sure he had heard wrong. What could happen in a church? Blood surged into his ears. He yanked kids aside to open the door. They all bolted out behind him into the band of light from the room. "Get back!" he yelled, pounding the wall for a light switch that wasn't there. "Mom?" He hung uncertain again, knowing he couldn't run to hunt her with fourteen little kids following him. "Back, back, back!" He swept them into the nursery and slammed the door. A mistake. He was in the dark hall, and inside, half the kids began to cry. In two

21

minutes one of them would figure how to turn the knob. He lunged off through the darkness, straight into Annie.

"Good grief!" she gasped. "What else is going to hit me?"

"Hit you?" He recoiled into a wall from their collision. Her hand took his and he followed her clopping sandals around a jog in the hall. "Hit you! What?"

Her hand turned loose and flipped a light switch. He jumped backward. At his feet lay a huge hairy creature. Two eyes glared up from a heavy head, freezing him motionless.

Then he saw what it really was. He made a croak of astonishment. Beyond it, lighted, was a storage room full of toys and books. "A big *teddy bear* hit you?"

"Not a teddy bear. Teddy bears are cuddly. This is a monster," Annie said in a squeaky voice, "I'm sorry — I didn't mean to yell like that. But it startled the daylights out of me."

Stowe nudged it gingerly with his foot. It was one of those gigantic stuffed animals he had seen in stores, that were twice the size of the children people bought them for. "I reached my hand in to turn on the light and it fell right out on me. Against my face — "

He thought she was laughing. But she bent into her hands, making giggly sobs. "Hey," he said. "Hey. Mom." He gave the giant bear a shove and closed it up in the storeroom. "There. Back in its cage."

"The kids." She ran toward the nursery. "Wait. You go in. Let me pull myself together."

Stowe pushed slowly against a logjam of crying kids. He counted, and got thirteen. Frantically he counted

22

again. Fourteen. He knelt and tried to comfort the loudest ones. "Hey, I've come back. See? I'm right here, dummy doodles."

Annie came in, holding her pale face in a smile.

Stowe laughed. "Hey, it was just a toy."

Instead of laughing with him, her eyes filled with tears and she made the same crinkled face as the children. "I know." She looked funny, trying to keep her face calm for them while she cried. "Just — suddenly all the years of being scared of old dark buildings and basements and driving home at night on icy streets and being responsible for more little kids than I can take care of — it just all came together."

He didn't know what to say. It seemed sort of neat to him that she could wait until she had a lot to cry about and then do it all at once, like running all her errands in one trip to save gas.

She scrubbed her eyes. "I'm sorry," she said, sniffing. "All of a sudden I'm just tired of being brave."

He studied the reflection of her face in the window, aware that he hadn't really looked at her in a long time. He hadn't needed to — he had known he would see his mother, in old jeans and a sweatshirt, probably barefooted, fixing something, listening, grey-eyed.

He guessed he should have regretted all the times he had begged off helping with her nursery jobs. It had never occurred to him that she was scared of anything. She had always seemed so confident, even when they were moving into strange empty houses or poking around in the mountains or playing in parks at night. He had always felt safe and self-confident because she was.

23

"I never knew you weren't brave," he said.

"You weren't supposed to. I used to be brave. But it's taking me a long time to get my confidence back. I'm still scared to feel deeply about things. You know? Or trust." She smiled suddenly at his reflection beside hers. "Except you," she said.

In his mind he formed two sentences. *Your cousin Harold called just when we were leaving. He said your dad would like to see me.* He imagined that her eyes widened. *Just me. Not you.* In his imagining, her face dissolved into the rain on the window.

"Oh," she said. "I found crackers. The box must have shot out of my hand when we collided."

Stowe went out into the hall and spotted the carton lying just beyond the band of light. Back inside, the children surrounded him, waving like an octopus. He handed a cracker to each tentacle, then took one for Annie and one for himself. A hush spread across the room, filled with little gnawings and crunchings.

"The opium of the people," Annie said, smiling. Stowe smiled back, relieved, without the faintest idea what she meant. She was always quoting a book or song or someone's good advice from a time he didn't know. What mattered was that she looked happy again. Anything he might say to threaten that would have to wait.

The toys were stored. The worst of the crumbs had been scratched out of the carpet, and all the children had been carried away but one. The little doll-faced girl watched the door apprehensively, but nobody came for her.

When a grey-haired woman stuck her head in at the door, little doll-face started up, then sank back again into Annie's lap. "Oh, here you are," the woman said, holding out a thin sheaf of dollar bills. "Only one child tonight?"

"Fourteen," Annie said. She took the money and folded it uncertainly. "The two assistants didn't show. If my son hadn't helped me — " She gave Stowe a glance and he saw that she was trying to squeeze some pay for him.

"Oh, wasn't that sweet of him to volunteer?" the woman said, pinning him in a spotlight smile.

"Look," Annie murmured, "unless I can be sure of helpers next time, I'm afraid I can't — "

"Oh, we'll definitely have someone here to help you, dear," the woman said, disappearing out the door smile last.

The little doll-face, uncollected for the fifteenth time, began to shout, "I want my mama. Where's my *mama*?"

"Dead," Stowe said, too tired to care.

"Stowe!" Annie pressed him toward the door. "How about seeing if we left the light on in the storeroom?"

He slammed out into the hall, furious without reason at the woman, at the little girl's mother chatting away downstairs, at the skinny sheaf of bills his mother had put meekly into her purse. "Obscurity," he hissed, but that wasn't the word. "Obesity. Obscenity!"

The light was still on. He kicked the hulking bear so hard it hurtled into a stack of hymnbooks. He looked around, abruptly subdued, and restacked them.

Far away at the end of the corridor a strip of light showed under a door. Annie must have been looking there and left it on, he guessed, although she was usually a strict turner-offer. He peeped in, ready to dodge anything that fell out at him. To his surprise he found he had opened the door on a large shadowy balcony, and the light was glowing up from the main part of the church. He could see blue carpet barred with pews, and tall colored windows. At the organ a man with a bald spot silently gathered up sheet music.

Stowe eased nearer the balcony rail, into a kind of heavy air that he guessed must be reverence. I'm in the house of God, he thought. In the chaos of the nursery he hadn't quite made the connection.

He wondered if the organ peals, and the hymns, and all the prayers of burdened people went darting out on Sunday mornings, stained red and gold from their passage through the glass. Or did they never have to leave, because God was right there listening? Maybe the heaviness he felt was the weight of all those prayers imprisoned under the carved ceiling, being sorted, being answered.

The bald-headed man switched off a final light. In the darkness Stowe heard a door click. The windows slowly took the shape of grey rockets aimed at heaven.

Longing came up from the place where he had pushed his secret. He would like to say something, but he had never prayed so formally before. Usually his prayers were sudden desperate commands like, God, get me out of this, quick. Now, instead of an asking prayer, he wanted to make a telling prayer. But what did people say? Dear Father? He didn't feel that way about fathers.

He guessed most of the time people said, Oh my God.

"I want to make it up to my mother," he whispered.

"Like paying her back for taking care of me and all, and showing me the fun instead of the bad parts."

He glanced around, feeling overheard — but wasn't that what he wanted, to be listened to?

"She trusts me." It had frightened and touched him when she said that. "I can't let her down when I'm the only one she trusts. You know about my grandfather, what he did. I've got to make all that up to her." He followed the soaring windows to their arch. "Wouldn't it just be better not to tell her what her cousin Harold said? I can't go unless she does. Wouldn't that just make her sadder?" In the dark he breathed the prayer-heavy air. "I want to make up for my father, too. She's stuck with me, so it's only fair for me to take his place. I've got to do a better job than they did, and provide for her, and make her happy, and you know, protect her and build up her confidence. So I've got to be mature and understand things and all like that. So I'm promising. Honor bright. I promise to give her what they didn't."

He turned and groped for the door to the hall, breathing quickly because he wasn't sure, exactly, what they hadn't given her, that he had just promised to give.

The little doll-faced girl and her mother were disappearing down the stairs at the far end. He leaned against the door, feeling all used up. Annie came out of the nursery and looked up and down, rubbing her shoulders that always ached from holding children. As he went toward her light he knew he couldn't ever keep that fancy smart-ass promise. How could he provide for her? He couldn't even grow hair. How could he balance out the wrongs of those men in her life when he was too happy being young and dumb and cared-for to be a man himself?

When they went out into the rain-chilled darkness, Horseless was all alone in the yellow streetlight. The clouds had broken. "Stars," Annie breathed, and lifted her face to the sky.

She tiptoed through a puddle and got in. The door swung shut with a long croak of protest and failed to lock. She slammed it again. Stowe clamped his teeth. Piece of junk, he told it, feeling water ooze through the holes in his sneakers.

He told little stories in his mind, to anyone who asked. The garage was letting them use this old clunker while their Mercedes was being fixed. Sometimes he made it their Ferrari being fixed. But he never, even in his mind, admitted they had to get around in a sixteen-year-old pickup truck, or walk.

Just as he was opening his own door in disgust, a curl of paper under the pickup's wheel caught his eye. He knelt, forgetting the puddle, and touched it.

"Back up," he called. Annie stuck her head out. "Back up a foot. There's something under the tire."

"Oh, eek!" Annie cried. "Have I run over something?"

"Mom." He spread his hands to show serenity. "Just back up a foot — do you mind?"

She poked Horseless to life and eased it back. Stowe snatched the little slip of paper up into the streetlight's glare. A shiver flickered over him like mountain wind.

"What?" Annie begged. "Stowe, for heaven's sake, what?"

He wiped the paper on his shirt front. "Nothing much.

28

A small twenty-dollar bill." He heard her breath. Her head and hand came out the window. He felt a flash of regret as his treasure slipped from his fingers into hers.

"It is. It really is," Annie said. "One of the choir members, getting out of a car." She smoothed it, looking around. "Everybody's gone. Do you think a janitor might still be in there?"

"Mom," Stowe said incredulously. He got in the pick-up.

"Well, we need to turn it in, or something, Stowe. How would you feel if you'd lost it?"

"Mom." He grabbed it back before she rushed over and tacked it to the church door. "We parked on it. We saved it from washing down the sewer with the run-off."

She hesitated, staring at it. "But don't you think we ought to ask around?"

"That's stupid. Everybody we asked would say, 'Sure, I lost it.' "

"But it's not ours," she said again.

"No, it's not ours," he yelled, suddenly too tired to be superhuman. "While you were counting stars I was crawling around in a puddle and *I* found it. It's mine."

They sat in a silence so deep he could feel the clock on the dash making quick heartbeats. Just like a little house, she used to say. A clock, a radio. Water jug behind the seat, food in the glove compartment. Dear old Horseless Carriage is our little home-away-from-home. We're a two-headed turtle in a shell.

Annie said tightly, "I don't think I could feel good about myself."

"You don't have to." The brazenness dropped out of

him, leaving him sad. "Jeez, you were just asking where more money was coming from. Can't you say, Hey, thanks! without ruining it? Can't you just be glad?" His stiff fingers folded the twenty-dollar bill and put it in the pocket of his shirt.

Annie gazed at him a long time. He watched a car pass. He wiggled his wet toes. Horseless idled. Was she waiting for him to give it back? He wasn't going to. Another shiver chilled him as he realized what that money meant, if he kept it for his very own. It meant he had unexpectedly made the last move in a weary, private game he had been playing for a whole year. He had just won.

Suddenly she started off, lurching backward because she'd forgotten she was in reverse. The tailgate went *erk-erk* in a laugh. "Shut up," she said, and they went home.

# ❧ Two ❧

Annie had the table set for three when Stowe and Brownie heaved their bikes up on the porch and pitched the paper-route bags into the living-room closet. "Want to eat with us?" Stowe asked, in the ceremony they followed every Saturday morning.

Brownie made his round, Saint Bernard face look surprised. "Oh — well, sure, I might as well." Both his parents worked for the city, he had told Annie the first time he stayed, and weekends were when they caught up on their rest, or anyway on their recreation. When he'd yell, What's for breakfast? they'd yell through the bedroom door, Go study so you can go to college.

"I've got to mow the cat lady and the corner man," Stowe said, checking his 2-Do 2-Day notebook.

Brownie said, "I'll trim edges for you so we can get going on the dam."

Having Brownie made life better. An afternoon route was bad enough, but eighty-one newspapers splatting the sidewalk on Saturday and Sunday mornings was a real punch in the nose. Except that, most weekends, he found

31

Brownie waiting on the porch when he stumbled out at five o'clock. Sometimes even in the winter darkness, Brownie had the bales already cut, and half the papers folded, with the inserts added and everything. That way, the breakfast invitation was earned, and they could celebrate being up and ahead of everyone, with apple sauce and waffles.

"What dam?" Annie asked.

They flashed each other looks, sorry she had overheard. "Creek," Stowe said. "After I do both yards. We're just going to pile some rocks up and see if we can make a deep spot."

He didn't want to sound weird, saying they'd been seized by the idea of holding back something that by the laws of nature couldn't be held back.

Annie said, "There's an old iron bar behind the fence that Sir Landlard probably wouldn't mind your using. If you put it back. Good for levering boulders."

Stowe went to get it, glad that Annie was still a little formal after their difference of opinion over the twenty-dollar bill the night before. Otherwise she would very likely have asked all about their plans and caused them to teeter along the edge of the truth more than they were teetering already.

"What if she decides to come and see the dam?" Brownie asked as they drank the cat lady's apple juice, sprawled on her half-mowed lawn.

Stowe gazed up into the cat lady's tree. Life had been so simple, before, when he was little. He told Annie what he was planning to do, and she said, Fine, and he did it. Or she said, No, and explained why not. And he didn't do it.

There had been an orderly safeness in the boundaries of those days that was as satisfying in its way as making his own decisions was now. He almost missed it.

"Maybe she won't have time," he said. What worried him more than the dam was how he could get to the bank without having Annie ask questions or Brownie ask to go along. Actually, a sliver of him hoped he wouldn't have time to go until Monday, so he could think the whole thing out better.

They were finishing the lawn on the corner of the block when a motorcycle tore past. The face of the skinny kid in front was a blur through the windscreen of his helmet, but the blond girl clinging to him flashed them a big smile and waved.

"Was that our Karla?" Brownie asked. "I thought she was visiting her dad this summer."

They both waved back, more at the fancy bike than at her.

"Who is that jerk?" Stowe asked. "Wish a cop would bust him. Knobbies aren't street-legal. No lights, no muffler . . ." He trailed off, admiring the lawbreaker with the same intensity as Brownie.

They watched the motorcycle bank at the far corner of the block. The front body canted at the same angle as the bike, but the back one leaned the opposite way, frantically trying to stay upright. A squeal floated back to them.

"She just stayed two months," Stowe said. Karla lived across the street. That made her the nearest thing to a girl-next-door he'd ever had, but they hadn't seen much of each other during the last months of school. Then suddenly she was gone. He had missed the times when summer

33

storms came up while her mother was at work, and Karla came bounding across the street to sit on their couch with a pillow over her head. "She looks different," he said. "Her dad let her get her ears pierced."

"Oh, pathetic," Brownie said. "Two more holes in her head."

"And even more junk on her face than before. Eyelashes like on a camel. She looks like she's dipped in batter, ready to cook."

Brownie gazed at the empty street. "Looks like she was really cooking today."

"I invited her to go on the picnic," Stowe said, wondering how that would set with Brownie. "She's going to bring dessert."

Brownie came to attention. "All right! What's she bringing?"

"Those big huge peanut butter marshmallow cow-patty kind of cookies she made us at Christmas." Stowe smiled in anticipation too. Annie had promised them an all-day picnic up at Sutherland's Camp. But that was next Saturday. This was dam day. He headed the old power mower toward home on its back wheels. "Let's get down to the creek and get to work."

A long sheet of plastic had given them the idea. They had found it blown against a pile of rocks right at the spot where the noisy creek squeezed itself up to flow under Apex Street. For years they had walked through the dim tunnel, reading the comments painted on its concrete walls, through water that never poured more than ankle-deep along the concrete bottom. At the sight of the plastic they had been struck with the best idea of the summer.

"Us against gravity," Stowe had whispered, awed by the idea. "If we took rocks in there, nobody could see us and say stop. Right in there against those sewer pipes or whatever they are that cross the tunnel."

"And then the plastic laid against the rocks," Brownie had whispered back, as though they were planning a prison break just three feet from a guard. "Stowe, we could dam that whole tunnel into a swimming pool!"

They were heading for Apex Street with a shovel and the iron bar when Karla yelled, "Hi," from her porch and came down to block the sidewalk where they had to pass.

They studied her. She had been as cute as a cupcake when they first knew her, but they couldn't get used to the frosting she kept adding. Brownie said, "What's stuck to your ears — ticks?"

"Ho ho, Brownie," she said. She touched the little gold pins in her lobes, and turned to Stowe. "I'm ready."

He had just bluffed his way past Annie, and still felt guilty. "Ready for what?" He wasn't about to share dam-building with her.

"The go-cart. You promised I'd get to steer when I got home."

Stowe shuffled. "I did?" She looked so different that he felt artificial, too, wondering if she saw changes in him.

"We've got a job," Brownie said, trying to make the shovel look professional.

"Come on, you guys said you'd let me, way back in the spring." Karla caught their hands and dragged them back toward Stowe's house. They exchanged glances again, behind her, to check how far they were willing to be delayed by a pretty girl fresh off a Kawasaki who wanted to ride their go-cart.

"Maybe one run from the top of the hill?" Stowe asked.

Brownie brought them to a stop in the middle of the street. "How many cookies are you making?"

Karla appraised him from under her carefully corkscrewed bangs. "How does five dozen hit you?"

Brownie whooped. "Give that little lady *two* runs and I'll push."

They got the go-cart from under the high back porch. It was a long clumsy job that Stowe had built himself, not counting a few weeks' help from Annie. Brownie shoved it to the top of the gently sloping street, panting and wagging. Stowe and Karla eased themselves down between the plywood sides, and Karla took the loop of cable she would steer with. It had never occurred to him before to wonder where to put his legs.

"Are you sure you know what to do?" he asked, looking at her little red-nailed fingers curled around the cable.

"Left for left, right for right — do I have to be a mechanical genius?" She made the front wheels wiggle. "Go, Brownie. Let's squirt dirt."

Brownie checked for cars and pushed off. He leaped on the back, crouching above Stowe's head. The go-cart began to grumble down the street, gaining speed with every clack of its wheels. Stowe grabbed Karla around the waist, feeling fewer bones than when they used to roughhouse on her lawn, and braced his knees on either side of her. She veered sharply to miss a beer can, and they all swayed sideways as she tried to compensate.

36

"More gradual," Stowe yelled. She squealed, missed a parked car by three inches, and swerved into the middle of the street again. They were flying. Her hair tickled Stowe's mouth. Up above them, Brownie tilted like a dog at a car window, gulping air, his hair flattened to his forehead.

"What if a car comes?" Karla shouted.

"Pull over."

"What?" she exclaimed.

"Pull over." Stowe realized his mistake. "*If* a car comes!" But he was too late. She gave the cable a left tug that could have uprooted a tree. They swayed toward a curb, then flopped in the opposite direction as she jerked right. Through the rush of wind Stowe heard the parting screech of plywood and nails. He tried to catch Karla's elbows, but she yanked again. Brownie toppled over Stowe's shoulder, grabbing at empty space, and disappeared. Stowe glanced back and saw him sitting in the street on a little platter of plywood that had been the rear of the go-cart.

The cart rocketed over a low curb, through a skinny new hedge, and out again in a sudden loop, spraying leaves. The jolt of hitting the curb again bounced Stowe out the back. He heard a rip as he slid across the remaining nails, and for a moment he felt street grit sandpapering the seat of his jeans. As Karla jerked again he slid completely off and watched her shoot obliquely across the street and ram the cart between the wheels of a parked van.

He leaped up, his bottom smarting, and ran to her. She was lying flat under the van like a mechanic on a little creeper. Stowe pulled the cart out and stared down. A leaf had stuck to Karla's forehead like a green kiss. Brownie came puffing up. "Is she — " They bent over her, taut with misgiving.

Karla's eyes popped open, round and dazzled. She made a Sleeping Beauty smile and sat up. "When are you guys going to learn to ride this thing?"

"Karla, you freak," they shouted together in relief. Brownie waved the plywood from the end of the cart. "He meant *if a car comes*, pull over!"

"Well how was I to know?" Karla yelled back. "I couldn't see through you blockheads to tell if a car was coming." She stood up, dusting herself. Stowe reached to help, and stopped. It seemed natural to run his hands along her new slopes the way he would examine a new tool or model rocket, or something, but he didn't think it would seem natural to anybody else. The kiss fell off her brow. "What if a truck was about to run us over and I hadn't done what he said?"

Stowe wagged the broken front wheels. "A truck might have been an improvement." He wished he could tell, without feeling, how much the rip in his jeans had exposed.

"Oh, boy," Brownie bellowed, "I can hardly wait till you learn to drive. Clear the streets, folks. Killer Karla is loose."

"You'll be begging to ride in my hot-pink Corvette with white fur upholstery," Karla said.

Stowe looked at Horseless parked down the street. He could almost drive it already. Annie let him start it up on winter mornings, after he'd brushed snow and scraped the windows, but the thought of taking a driving test in that clanking old tank made his stomach dip. In his mind he turned to the examiner who sat beside him, matching his small contemptuous smile. Airily he said, For a nice gesture I promised my grandfather I'd take my test with the same truck he used for his.

I was just saying that, he told the man in his mind. Horseless is all we can afford. And I never promised my grandfather anything. "Money," he said aloud, clamping his hand over his rip. "I need money for things!"

Karla and Brownie looked him up and down in wonder. Karla asked, "What's the matter with him? I didn't know you could get a concussion at *that* end."

Stowe grabbed the cable and towed the wobbling go-cart toward home, feeling fresh air through the rip at every step.

Brownie loped after him, calling back, "Lock your door at night, Killer. We'll get you for this." He remembered the cookies and stopped. "After the picnic, naturally."

They watched her laugh and run home, bouncing where she'd never bounced before.

Stowe sighed. "Should have known." The bent axle grated like fingernails on a blackboard.

"Yeah," Brownie agreed. "Always. Calamity Karla. Like that Fourth of July, when her marshmallow caught on fire."

"And she whipped her stick back and the marshmallow flew off and stuck to my mom." They had to grin.

"And the time playing hide and seek when she hid in

the garbage can." They looked back, half-forgiving, but she had gone in.

By noon the water in the tunnel under Apex Street was knee-high. They squished home sopping wet and threw sandwiches together. Annie was at the store getting the batting for a quilt and the house was eerily quiet. The most beautiful thing about weekends was that Yetta and Tyler didn't come. Annie scooped all the kid-junk, the toys and rubber sheets and little plastic glasses, out of sight, and scrubbed the main smears off walls and furniture and sometimes ceiling, and yelled, Free at last! as she set all her breakables out again.

They ate back at the creek edge, warming away their goosebumps while the water slowly rose out of its banks among the weeds. Through a gap in the foothills they could see, far up on the second range of mountains, the white, cupped snow patches where all the creeks began.

"Is that where we're going, Saturday?" Brownie asked.

Stowe let his mind slide past the overlapping mountains, each one a different shade of distance, and stop in the warm, still meadow of Sutherland's Camp. For one long breath he could smell pines and new air. "Yeah. Over behind that peak with the knob on top. It takes about an hour, the way Horseless pulls hills."

"How come your mom knew about it?"

"She used to go there in the summers with her folks. It used to be a really old resort, with little cabins and a big dining hall and all. But when we went up to find it, nothing's left but some foundations. I guess it burned." He hesitated. The rest got a little personal to share, even

40

with Brownie. Annie had broken into tears because the place was gone where she had spent the happiest days of her life, and Stowe, watching her, had silently vowed to buy that spot and build a house there.

"That's when things were different with her dad," he said, hoping Brownie would answer in a way that would let him casually talk about the phone call. On the other hand, he hoped he wouldn't, because Brownie would probably blurt out, Jeez, go see the old dude — maybe he wants to leave you everything in his will! and he'd be more confused than ever.

Brownie said, "Are we going to cook out, all three meals?"

"Sure," Stowe answered, grateful for the postponement. "If we can get up and get going early enough. When she says all-day picnic, she means dark to dark."

"I'll be at your house at four," Brownie said. "We can have the papers done in thirty minutes if your mom drives us and we both throw."

"And then another thirty minutes to pry Karla out of bed."

"Really — and then forty-five minutes for her to put on her face."

"At least," Stowe agreed, not sure it had been a good idea to invite her. Then he remembered. "Hey, there's this old, slimy mine up there. We can take her in and pretend to lose her." They grinned peacefully, savoring the idea. He sat up. "I've got a flashlight. But if you've got any fresh batteries you better bring some. We don't want to *really* wander around lost in that sucker."

They eased themselves into the icy water and dug out a

rock that had been too heavy to tackle before lunch. Together they struggled with it into the tunnel. In the dimness they hoisted the chunk of granite to the top of the dam, and went out for more.

"We're dumb," Brownie said an hour later. "What we need now is pieces of lumber. Plywood. Lighter stuff we can lean against these pipes and put the plastic over."

"And you know what else? Inner tubes to float on. So at least the top half of us won't need to freeze."

They splashed out into the afternoon glare and headed for Brownie's house. Annie always had better tools, but Brownie's folks had a lot of really super junk and couldn't care less when it disappeared. They patched up two old truck tubes and pumped them into huge black doughnuts at the station on the corner. With the tubes around their necks they were able to carry enough lumber scraps to build the dam as high as their heads.

They could actually see water rising on the dark walls after they had wedged the wood above the rocks and faced it with their plastic sheet. It slowly swallowed up the hearts and swastikas and who-plus-whos and the brave-scared dirty words that kids had practiced writing in there where no one could see. They lay across their inner tubes, their numbed bottoms sagging through the holes, and paddled busily back and forth, adjusting boards and tucking the plastic around leaks. They could look over the dam's top and see only a shallow stream wandering along the bottom toward the square of light at the other end of the tunnel.

"We're doing it!" they exclaimed to each other. Stowe

floundered off his tube and stood in the water to test its depth. It had risen to his armpits. He could feel its force against the thick barrier they had raised. Occasionally a rock settled or a board groaned, and they held their breath, staring into each other's blue-lipped face, until they were sure the dam was holding.

"You think we can build it strong enough to last the rest of the summer?" Brownie asked. "With just a real skinny spillway at the top? We could swim in here!"

"Or build a raft. Hey. Charge admission."

"Tunnel of love," Brownie giggled.

"Unless some cop drives by on Apex and sees all that water backed up out there." Stowe squinted out into the glare. "Oh, jeez," he added. A head was looking at them from the top of the tunnel entrance, and even upside down he could tell it was Annie, hanging over the edge.

They paddled out with their wrinkled hands and looked up at her. She righted herself and hung her feet off into space. The water almost reached them. On either side, water lapped across the newly drowned grass and bushes of the creek bank.

"The Noah Brothers, I presume," she said. "Quite a flood you've got here."

They glanced at each other, confused because she didn't seem angry or shocked at finding them there. "Yeah, how about this?" Stowe said, looking back. He felt safe enough to say, "Almost to our chins."

"An engineering marvel," Annie said. "I wish I could see it, but you've made the lake so deep I'd need a boat."

Brownie got his courage back. "Want to use my tube?"

"Thanks, but I get seasick easily." Her eyes studied the street and the new shoreline, and came back to them. "You two are freezing."

"We've been working too hard to get cold," Stowe said, trying to keep his shivers from showing. "We must have moved a ton of rocks. Big ones. It's a real dam."

"I can see that," Annie said, gazing instead into his eyes.

"Tomorrow we might build a raft." He threw his cold hands out to indicate the grand expanse it could float in.

"Afraid not," Annie said. She smiled at them. "The dam's got to go."

They swiped the water, trying to keep themselves stationary, to be sure they had heard right. Stowe took a drowning breath. "Why?" He gave the end of the word a curlique to say he was going along with her joke but would rather laugh outright.

"Because, first, it's probably against the law. Isn't this city property? If a flash flood brought a lot of extra water through here, it could damage the street, or the tunnel, or wash out these banks. Don't you know about mountain rains? And aren't some pipes running across the tunnel in there? They could rupture."

Brownie let himself drift slowly toward the tunnel, his face carefully blank. Stowe ached to turn away from her in the same way. "It's not going to rain. Boy, if people thought up everything bad that could happen, they'd be afraid to get out of bed."

"Stowe," she said. "Kids are allowed to play here because the water's usually shallow. Imagine a little kid discovering a big wide lake to explore. It's too risky."

He fixed a grin on his face to hide the dropping-away hollowness that her reasoning made in him. The fact that she was probably right about dangers he hadn't even thought of made her authority impossible to accept.

He whirled his tube and stroked it toward the tunnel, churning the water until it lapped and glinted in anger. In the dimness Brownie drifted close, mumbling sadly, "Jeez, all that work."

"Sorry," Annie called. They heard her sigh. "Could have saved yourselves. Could have told me honestly what you were planning to build. I would have stopped you flat, right there."

"That's why we didn't," Brownie mumbled to the glare.

"I know," Annie said. "So, okay, you guys have had your fun. It's a beautiful job, it really is. I'm sorry. But take it down."

Stowe paddled out again. "Why? If you came along and some other kids had built it, you wouldn't tell them what to do."

Annie stood up. "You're not some other kid. You're my kid." Stowe saw for the first time that she had brought oatmeal cookies for them in a plastic bag. Her face was set. She said, "Better begin to let the water through, slowly. Then clear out the tunnel."

"But it's not hurting anything."

"All the rocks. The wood. Bring home whatever you brought." She climbed up to the Apex Street sidewalk. "Okay?" she asked firmly.

They paddled in silence, making their tubes swirl, glancing anxiously at each other as they came face to face.

45

"Pitiful," Brownie murmured. "All that work."

Stowe lifted his shriveled toes out of the water. With one eye closed he sighted past them at Annie walking out of sight down Apex Street. He made a small trigger-pulling gesture with his finger. "Pow," he said. He laughed suddenly, feeling strange. "Hey," he said uneasily, "we would have cleaned it up anyway. Wouldn't we? When we decided to take it down. We weren't going to leave it in there forever." The hollowness in him grew. Now all at once he was sounding as if he agreed with Annie automatically. Like a puppet nodding because she had wriggled her wrist. But what else could he do when what she said made sense? He was used to keeping things right with her. It felt good to be together on things with her.

"Don't you ever argue with her?" Brownie asked, making what looked like a sun-squint.

"Sure. Didn't I argue with her? I argued with her." Stowe tried to think what he had said, but the words blurred.

"Not so you could tell," Brownie said, still making the sun-grimace. "I mean a real yelling and cussing argument — the saying-you'll-leave-home kind."

Stowe kept his face expressionless. Leaving home was the last thing he would ever want to do. "You have that kind?"

"Once a week. At least." Brownie's grin faded. "She sure bosses you around a lot."

Stowe stroked back into the dark tunnel, trying to think if she really did boss him. Maybe Brownie was just embarrassed at being caught. Or maybe she did. It hadn't

46

seemed like bossing. More like explaining something they hadn't thought of. A discussion. So they could decide. But maybe she did.

"She expects me to do the right thing," he said defensively. "Hey, I like doing crazy things as much as you do. But she expects me to be responsible and all that."

"Big wow," Brownie said.

Stowe paddled up to the dam. His hand could feel the plastic molded to the rocks by the water's pressure. He said, "If we can tilt this board and push rocks out here the whole thing will go at once."

Brownie came slopping up close enough to bump tubes. "She said slow."

"Just one push, I bet." Stowe tested an edge of the plastic, trying to ignore the butterflies in his stomach. A little spout of water dropped through the opening he had made. "One good push," he said.

Brownie hesitated. Suddenly he braced himself. "You really want to?" He banged a board. "Okay! Tidal wave!" They ripped at the plastic. Water jetted, slurping through the crevices they had exposed. Small rocks began to clatter to the tunnel floor.

"Kick!" Stowe ordered. He maneuvered his tube, lunged at the piled rocks, and went spurting backward from the impact.

"Stowe," Brownie said sharply, "if it all goes at once, we're going to go with it."

"Riding the rocks!" Stowe yelled. He caught the cold fat pipe that crossed the tunnel, and knocked out a board they had wedged against it. With a rumble the rocks began to shift. He felt a surge of water carrying him

47

forward, and braced his legs stiff to keep from crashing into the dam. Suddenly in the dimness the water tilted and dropped into a trough. His inner tube flipped out from under him and his head fell back into an icy rushing gloom.

When he rose the rocks were tumbling. He fought against the pull of suppressed water breaking free. With a grinding surge he and Brownie and the tubes and lumber rode over the pipes and poured along the tunnel floor.

Rocks clattered around them. As he grabbed for his tube something bashed him into the tunnel wall. He saw Brownie sweep past. Then the water scooped Stowe on, coughing and flailing. Behind him the rocks cracked together and grated along the cement. He saw the end of the tunnel jolt and grow. The plastic slithered past, humped like a sea monster, and was beaten down by sliding rocks.

He thought to Annie, Okay, this is what you wanted.

Abruptly he rolled to a stop against a boulder. Water still streamed past him and swirled out into the creek bed. In the glare of the tunnel's end he could see Brownie staggering toward him against the flow, wearing his inner tube like a ballet skirt and beaming with delight.

"Wow," Brownie yelled, sloshing into the tunnel where Stowe was beached. "Jeez! We nearly killed ourselves. A wall of water. Look where it carried that boulder." Diluted blood was trailing off his knee but he was too happy to notice. "A solid wall of water. Must have been. Wow."

A chill shuddered through Stowe. He parted his sagging hair and gazed back into the rock-strewn tunnel. The water still rushed, but calmly now, carrying their backed-up lake across the rubble of the dam. After all their efforts, gravity had won. Now, too late, he stiffened with the apprehension he should have felt before he risked so much. *Think ahead*, he could almost hear Annie order. We don't have enough money to be stupid.

He felt danger like a cold wind on his skin. Close call. A really stupid close call. Even if he had just cracked a finger, or something — there would have gone the twenty dollars that meant so much. And if he had bashed his head in, Annie wouldn't even have known to look for the money in the baseball mitt where he had stuffed it last night. Or to look behind the train poster. Or in the model rocket, or the centerfold of the magazine he kept in his winter-clothes drawer.

He glanced back at Brownie. "Hey. That didn't take long, did it?" He stood up in a burst of thankfulness, testing to see if all his arms and legs worked. His shoulder throbbed where he had hit the tunnel wall, and the skin was missing from one elbow, but his main sensation was a swept-clean calmness like the water. A balance. He had done what Annie asked, because she had been right, but he had done it his way. He had had the final say. It was worth some skin. Brownie was right to whoop and grin — they had surrendered to gravity in one whopping glorious flood.

They limped downstream and found Stowe's inner tube washed up on a sand island. Back in the tunnel they rolled the biggest boulders out, and gathered the bits of wood and plastic that had hung up on the rocks. The little lake they had created had become a muddy mess of debris and bent weeds. Brownie scrubbed his goosebumpy arms, and looked around with a mixture of awe and sadness. "Wow. It was big. Nobody's going to believe how big."

They dragged all their stuff to Stowe's house, and sprinted to the bathroom, dripping and shivering. In the tub they fought to stand under the hot water. Slowly their blue lips changed color, and their scraped skin began to sting.

"How you going to explain all these?" Brownie asked as they pasted bandages over their injuries.

Stowe studied their two faces in the mirror. A passing rock had taken a nick out of his chin, and Brownie had a cut lip. "I'll just tell her," he said, recognizing pride behind the calmness of his eyes. "We pulled it down too fast. It broke and we went with it. You give the orders and you take the risks."

Something dropped softly out in the hall, and Annie's voice said through the door, "Here's some dry clothes. Things for you, too, Brownie. Wring your wet stuff and hang it on the line. Mop where you dripped, coming in." They nodded to each other, rolling their eyes. "I've got five minutes to run buy some thread before the store closes."

Stowe froze with his fingers in the bandage box. Store closes! The bank was twenty minutes away by bike. He couldn't possibly make it. Now it would be Monday before his long game could finally end.

When they passed through the kitchen on their way to the clothesline, he saw the cookies waiting on a plate.

# ❧ Three ❧

Stowe diced his sunny-sided egg into four bites, wondering how he could get up and go to his room. It was silly, because other times when he was doing something ordinary he just got up and went in. But today was different. He felt watched, even though Annie was too busy to look up.

"Okay, Yetta-bug," she said impatiently. "Eat your cereal before it gets soggy." She was holding Tyler in her lap at the table because he still cried on Monday mornings for his dad.

Yetta's mother always left a package of cereal when she dropped Yetta off in the mornings, in case Yetta decided to join them for breakfast. Annie called the sugary stuff Cloy-Cloys, and usually managed to lose it or drop it, so she could feed Yetta the oatmeal or wheat germ they were having. But today, after a weekend of backsliding, Yetta had insisted on her own. She sat on four used-book-store volumes of the encyclopedia, patting the glittering flakes to mush.

"Tyler toast," Annie coaxed. She offered Tyler a bite

51

heaped with mashed egg. His mouth popped open, then closed just as the fork reached it. Food rolled down his front into Annie's lap like the tunnel rocks.

Stowe took his plate to the sink, moving twice as slowly as he wanted to. He sauntered out of the kitchen, and tiptoed with great jerky steps to his room. Should he shut the door? He never did. It would look strange. Besides, it wasn't that big a thing, really. Except to him.

He reached into the thick padded thumb of his mitt and pulled out the twenty-dollar bill. It had dried in a curl. He smoothed it silently, and opened a drawer. The magazine fell open where the lump was. He took out thirteen one-dollar bills, leaving the centerfold lady bare-ass, and laid them crossways on the twenty. From the cylinder of a rocket, where the parachute should have been wadded, he slid a roll of five-dollar bills. Nine of them. Mowing money. Crossways the others. Seventy-eight dollars.

"Stowe," Annie called. He froze, his fingers extended to take a tack from the corner of the train poster. If he didn't answer she might think he was in the bathroom. Silently he peeled two taped ten-dollar bills off the poster back. His ears began to throb with excitement. Ninety-eight. Paper-route bonuses at Christmas, just when he had sunk all his future pay into a used bicycle.

Out of a jar of dried-up salmon eggs he took eight quarters. That was it. For the first time in his life he held one hundred dollars in his hands.

"Stowe," Annie yelled louder.

"Yeah? What?" He stuffed it all into his pockets, smoothed the excitement off his face, and went to her.

"Could you fix the swing so they can play out back this morning?"

"Do I have to?" He started to say there was more cleaning up to do at the tunnel, but he had never lied very well. "I was going to ride my bike awhile. Can't they wait an hour? I'll fix it when I get back, first thing."

Yetta suddenly stood up on her chair and pointed imperiously at Stowe's glass with her spoon. "Stowe, get back here and drink your milk before it gets soggy."

Annie burst out laughing. Tyler copied her, letting another mouthful of egg bounce down his front. Stowe laughed, too, thankfully, gulped his milk and plunged out before his luck changed.

The breeze on his skin as he pedaled was like all of summer touching him, warm in the sun, cool in tree-shade, as it poured down the mountainsides. The bank clock said he had made the trip in seventeen minutes.

He stood in line at the walk-up window. What if he had to prove it was his money and not stolen? What if they said his mother had to sign something first? It felt strange not to have her there, or Brownie. He wasn't quite sure why this was a moment he wanted to experience alone. But it was.

At last he faced the teller through the glass. The sliding drawer popped out at him. He wet the inside of his mouth and stretched to reach the talking-hole. "A hundred-dollar bill," he said.

The teller leaned closer, looking mystified.

With a thud he remembered he hadn't given her his money. He emptied his pockets into the drawer. His little

2-Do 2-Day reminder book fell in with the bills, and he grabbed for it as the drawer glided shut. The drawer lurched out again, releasing his nipped fingers. The man behind him laughed as the drawer finally jerked forward like someone learning to drive.

With an exasperated smile the teller gathered his money and thumbed it rapidly into piles. She wrote something down. Then her hand came up with a single bill in it. She popped it like a little wet dishtowel to be sure another bill wasn't stuck to it, and sent it out to him in the drawer. He thought of Annie at the supermarket, trying to make two tens separate into more money.

"There you are," the teller said, as if it happened every day. It did, he guessed, to lots of people. He took the bill and his notebook and backed out of line. Benjamin Franklin. Smiling faintly. Stowe smiled back. A penny saved is a penny earned.

He folded Ben neatly in half and put the bill in his pocket. People in line were eying him, some curiously, some with smiles. He pedaled around the corner and stopped in the next alley to take it out again. Money.

He bet he was absolutely the only kid in town holding a hundred-dollar bill at that moment. It gave him the more-than-enough sense of security that people probably got from a gun, or a fancy car, or being the best at something. He was special. He had saved for a year to know this feeling, collecting dollars a dribble at a time after the expenses of his bike and the paper-route bags and the gas for the mower and his school supplies. It might have been months longer, if that gift from the street hadn't suddenly made it happen. Holding a crisp hundred-dollar bill made up for all the secondhand clothes and all the times of pretending he wasn't interested when his friends went to movies or bought junk to eat.

He rode home down the quiet side streets, grinning to himself, his chin cocked high.

"I love it!" he yelled at an empty corner. Power pulsed from his fingertips. His stomach giggled. *Rich*, his jeans whispered as he pumped up a hill. *Rich, rich, rich*.

He was back in his room before he realized he didn't know what he was going to do with a hundred-dollar bill.

Hiding just wasn't safe enough. Not with Yetta and Tyler poking around and his mother having sudden cleaning spells. He wanted to be able to see it and touch it — that was the whole point of bringing it all together in one mass fortune.

Out his window he could see Annie with her brace and bit, boring holes in a board for a swing seat. Yetta and Tyler squatted beside her, being patient. Stowe revolved, staring at the walls of his room. He didn't have all day. Where?

Then it came to him. A solution so simple it was audacious. He found his thumbtacks and stuck his money to the wall. He took some play-money bills from his Rich Millionaire game and tacked them beside it. In his treasures he found a peso he had traded a model for, and added it to his display.

Yetta came bounding in with the swing board clutched to her chest. Annie followed, holding the rope like reins. She said, "Ah, you're back. I was about to climb the tree."

"I'll do it," he said, carefully not looking at anything in particular.

She glanced out the window. "Grrr, the postman keeps snubbing us. I was hoping . . ." Her eyes swept past the display, stopped, and returned. "Good grief. What's all that?"

He made a hearty laugh. "What — my counterfeit collection? You've seen it before, haven't you, my peso and stuff? I got it from the kid that his father has the coin shop."

Annie got Yetta and the swing ropes untangled. "Well, I'm not an expert on hundred-dollar bills, but that one looks almost too real to be funny money."

He laughed again, a moment too long, suddenly uncomfortable at the trustful way she had accepted another one of his half-truths. "Yeah, really," he agreed. "I thought maybe it looked a little too green."

"Money can't look too green," she said, staring out again at the spot the mailman had passed. It took Stowe a moment to realize that she had been hoping for another Aunt Fritzi letter to tell her how her dad was.

"Get off my bed!" he told Yetta.

"It's my bed," she said.

"It's not." She took her naps there, and he resented it. Even with the rubber sheet spread for her, he expected to feel a damp spot every night. She glared at him, tucking herself protectively against Annie's leg. He guessed it was confusing to have two beds and two homes and two of everything. Two mothers.

Annie said, not even hearing them, "Surely she would have called, to let us know, if . . ."

Stowe jammed his hands into his empty pockets, and let his eyes sweep past the hundred dollars he didn't want to share with her. He could feel one of those little cartoon angels on one shoulder, and a devilish one on the other, poking him with a little fork. There was too much to think about. He needed time to lie on his bed, staring back at Ben Franklin and mulling the power that a slip of paper gave him.

"Maybe I ought to call her," Annie said, automatically smoothing Yetta's hair with anxious strokes. "Just for a minute tonight, when the rates are cheaper."

He thought, Why don't I just say here's a hundred bucks — let's go *see* how he is. But that wouldn't work. He had been asked for, and she hadn't. That stupid call had complicated everything. What if she called and Aunt Fritzi asked her, Have you decided? Are you sending Stowe?

He said, "Why do you keep on letting him mess up your life? You ought to just turn him off like a light bulb and never give him a chance to hurt you anymore."

She looked sad. "Hey. If I were in the hospital, I'd like to know that someone cared enough about me to call."

"I'd care," he said.

Annie took his head between her palms and gazed into his eyes with a tight-pressed little smile of love and gratitude that wrenched his heart.

Karla came out to sunbathe in her front yard while Stowe was folding papers. She waved, but her radio was blaring too loudly to yell over. He stuffed the grubby bags hanging on his handlebars, glancing over each time the pink bikini rotated in the sun. He felt self-conscious, wondering if people were watching him watch. Actually, it was the situation he was studying. If she had changed so much, he must have changed, too, without noticing. Which was scary. On the other hand, if he hadn't changed, he had to be the only person his age in the world stalled like an old car while everyone else was burning rubber getting past the awkwardness and ignorance and on with living. He was never going to catch up with Karla. He wished it wasn't a race at all, and they could all stand still, the way it had been.

He had an extra paper. He took it over and dropped it on her head. She raised up on one elbow and smiled. The radio throbbed. She opened the paper and read her horoscope while her fingers teased her earlobes.

"What was it like?" he asked. "Visiting your dad?"

"Dull." She read the funnies. "Except when he bought me clothes. That was fun. I came home with tons of stuff."

He wondered what it felt like, playing people off against each other. "When your dad let you pierce your ears — I guess that was a surprise."

"When I got home?" Karla laughed. "My poor little mother threw a double-decker screaming fit. But she was a tad too late to do anything about it."

He thought, Doesn't it seem strange, to poke holes in your ears? Now you're stuck with them, all the rest of your life. What if you change your mind, someday, about how you felt a long time ago? Like my grandfather.

He was sorry he had come over. He stood beside her, trying to read the funnies upside down, not quite sure how to leave.

"Stowe, you're blocking off the sun," she said. He

stepped back, into her radio. "Stowe, just go home, will you?"

He wished Brownie were there to make a smart crack. A sadness like someone's shadow moved across him. He went back across the street.

Tyler was up from his nap, banging the screen. Stowe let him out. Tyler plopped down, wet-bottomed, on a stack of papers and ate a rubber band. Stowe grabbed it like a robin's earthworm as it was going down. "No," he said. "Yucky." He dried his fingers, feeling watched. He thought of pitching a water balloon across the street, to cool Karla off, but things like that were more fun with Brownie, and besides, she heard her phone ring, and scampered in. To laugh about him with the Kawasaki King, probably. He sighed in the heavy August stillness for the way life was.

"Mom," he yelled. "Tyler's out here and I've got to go."

He could hear water running. "Stick him through the door," she yelled back. Usually she came out and helped fold papers, but he could hear the thump of the washing machine. Yetta, he guessed. She did a lot of throwing up. Sometimes she ran through her regular clothes and her emergency clothes and had to chug around in one of his T-shirts looking like the Seven Dwarfs while Annie washed everything.

He closed Tyler up in the house and wobbled heavily off on his bike. By the time he reached the corner, Annie had picked Tyler up and his screams had grated to a stop. Stowe drew a breath of relief and pulled steadily to the top of Third Street. He had two vacation-stops to remember, and people at one house looked like they were

59

packing to leave for good. He would have to catch them and collect before they moved away.

Papers in summer were a cinch. Winters sucked, because of the ice. He had taken so many falls that Annie finally said bad days automatically meant Horseless would do the sliding. At first he was embarrassed to kneel in the pickup bed, hucking papers at people's storm doors. But he got better at it, so good in fact that his customers began to call him the Porch-Putter, and he got less critical of Horseless with every snow.

The cat lady was waiting, stooped over on her porch with two apples in her little claw-shaped hands. Instead of pitching her paper, he knocked his kick-stand down and carried the paper up her walk. At the last moment, when he was close enough for her to see, he smiled.

"It's boiling out there — you need to wear a hat," she scolded him, for about the millionth time.

"I guess so," he agreed patiently, figuring she had grown up under a sunbonnet like the girl on the raisin box. She was okay. She said her son had wanted her to go to a rest home, but she had told him she wasn't tired. He took her apples and laid the paper on her warped knobby fingers. "What you need?"

"If you could just open a couple of cans for the cats," she said, tottering a little as she got herself headed indoors. He followed her to the kitchen and ran the can opener around the tuna she pointed out to him. "Oh, and Stowe, if you could just put a new roll of toilet paper on." She laughed and touched one of her useless hands with the other, gently, as if it were a child who couldn't help having something wrong with it.

As he went out, one of her cats stood up in the window to be petted. He stroked its orange coat, wondering what to do with the handful of hairs that came out. "I can cut your hedge tomorrow," he said from the sidewalk, letting fur drift unobtrusively through his fingers.

She nodded, smiling. "I couldn't do without you, Stowe."

He smiled back, wishing she could.

In the next block he was busily watching his own strong fingers sail papers expertly from gutter to doorstep when he collided with a puppy that galloped out between two parked cars. It gave one of those puppy howls that made it sound like it was dying, and at the same time began to wiggle and wag and crawl all over him with a face full of smiles. Stowe felt for a tag, but there was no collar in the ruff of rusty hair. He looked around. He had never seen it before, but somebody could have just brought it home from the pound. For the rest of the block he knocked and asked. Nobody knew who owned it.

"Hey," Stowe said at the corner, "go home. You can't come with me, I've got seven more streets to cross." The puppy sat down and agreed, then bolted after him as he started off. A car jerked to a stop for both of them. Stowe grabbed the puppy with one hand and pushed his bike with the other, wobbling with embarrassment. On the opposite corner he set the puppy down and towered over it. "Home," he ordered. "Get home." It was skinny. He had felt its ribs. It had little curly ears and a nose the color of liver. "Don't you come. No!" He sped away.

In the next block he threw a wild curve that clipped the flower right out of a pot sitting on somebody's porch step.

61

He stopped, wavered, and sped on, followed by the puppy gaining on him with every bound.

At the corner they eyed each other. Stowe looked up and down both empty streets. "You win," he said, and put the puppy into his sack.

But Annie didn't think so. "Oh, no," she groaned, looking up from floor-mopping as he unhooked the squirming sack. The puppy floundered out, kissed everyone in sight, and wet the floor in a burst of gratitude. Stowe took the mop she handed him.

"Oh, you sweet baby," Annie said, drawing Yetta and Tyler and the puppy into her lap in a heap.

"I was scared he was going to get run over," Stowe said hopefully. "I kept sending him back and sending him back."

"I know," she said. "It's okay." She and the puppy touched noses in understanding. "It's just that we can't keep him, Stowe. Sir Landlard rules."

He knelt with all of them on the damp floor and rubbed the puppy's head. "Maybe if we just sort of hid him?"

"Could we, the way Sir Landlard sneaks around? Remember last year when he came in and literally carried off the carpet while we were in town?"

"I know, but what if someone didn't want a puppy, and threw him out and he's homeless?"

She sighed. "Well, maybe better him than us. You like it here, remember. We're tempting fate already, taking in two more urchins than Sir Landlard bargained for." She popped a little row of sticktights that edged the puppy's ear. "Besides, this little guy may have a home already. Fix him something to eat while I call the Humane Society and that radio station that makes the lost and found announcements."

The puppy liked leftover macaroni, and peas, and the rest of Yetta's Cloy-Cloys. He had just gobbled them up when Yetta's mother came. Yetta had to be carried off wailing like an ambulance because she wanted to stay and watch the puppy eat one of the cat lady's apples.

By the time Tyler's dad had picked him up, Annie had called every place she could think of, and nobody seemed to have lost a rust-colored puppy. Stowe stroked it as it lay round-bellied and sleepy in the crook of his arm, holding himself numb. If nobody wanted it, it ought to be his. *He* wanted it. It was his little curly-eared lost baby — hadn't he found it? Nobody's rule ought to keep them apart.

"Hey," Annie said gently, "how about going back over your route and asking around. Okay?" She held out a red bandanna to use for a collar, and a coil of twine for a leash.

"It's not fair," he said. The feelings he thought were numb came bursting out. "It's not right! Jeez, I want to live where I can have any kind of pet I want. An elephant, if I want it."

"And lions and tigers and bears," Annie agreed, putting on her sandals.

She didn't understand how serious he was. "I mean it," he exclaimed. "Damn it, I'm going to have a piece of land that nobody can ever take away from me. *Ever.* And I can dig holes in it if I want to, and rearrange it and grow trees on it, and no stupid landlord can tell us what to do, or how long we can live there, or say move because we like dogs."

"I know," Annie said. She was always saying that, even when she couldn't possibly know. "I always had dogs and cats. I know it doesn't seem fair that you can't. When you're young and can't change things, it's a real bummer."

All at once he found a closer target than Sir Landlard for his anger. "You're not young," he said. "You could change things."

She knotted the bandanna around the puppy's neck. "How do you mean? Hey, I'd love that piece of land as much as you would. And I'd buy it in a minute. But what with, Stowe?"

He twitched his shoulders, angry that she wanted a specific answer when he was talking about unhappiness in general. "I don't know. Get a real job. Get married to somebody. How do I know?"

Annie's face went flat. She picked up the puppy and marched out the front door. Stowe followed. "I somehow had the impression that I've got a real job," she said stiffly. "I don't keep kids just to break the monotony of my empty days." She veered off across the street, walking so fast he almost had to jog. "I promised to keep Yetta till her mother gets her degree. And Tyler so his dad can keep custody. You know that."

He braced himself the way he did on her cranky days. He was in for a talking-to. He guessed he had hit a spot in her that ached like his bruised shoulder.

"That doesn't mean I don't like what I'm doing," she said in a calmer voice. "I love kids, and I love homemaking, and making the quilts and all that. I'm living the kind of life I want to live."

"Well, hooray for you," he said. "But we're poor."

"Well, damn it, I'm sorry it doesn't pay as much as being a grape on a TV commercial. But I wanted a job where I could watch you grow up. I wanted you to come home from school and yell my name, and get an answer."

He held his mouth shut. Brownie would have said right back at her, Hey, maybe I don't get answered, but I watch a twenty-five-inch TV till my folks get home.

She thought of something that made her irritated all over again. "And what do you mean — *get married to somebody* — like I was buying soap! Listen, marriage is a lot of time-consuming work."

"Didn't seem like you put much time into working for the one you had. Keeping it."

"I didn't want to keep it, Stowe. It was a big hopeless mistake. At first I thought I had failed some way or was guilty of something, but I wasn't. People make mistakes. Even trying hard, they make mistakes. So I don't choose to complicate my life that way anymore. Okay? I'm having too much fun."

"Okay!" He started to yell back, Maybe you're having fun, but I'm not! But that wouldn't be true. He was. He had things good, and ought to be grateful. Marrying somebody was the last thing he'd want her to do. He didn't know why he'd said it, except that it was what people expected, and they lived so crazy, and there was so much out there to want. "I just said you could change. You don't have to jump all over me."

"When what I'm doing doesn't seem right, I'll change. So stop trying to squish me into molds, and let me play by my own rules. Okay?" She cut through the deserted yard of the school he had gone to when they first came. "I know I'm not very aggressive anymore. I gave up being a shaker and a mover, and settled for just enduring, but I intend to hang on to what's important. Like being with you. Enjoying you. Living each day as it comes. Being unconventional, if that's what it takes. Crazy Annie."

It sounded like one of her quilt patterns. Little odd pieces going off in all directions. And a funny strong calico border around it all.

"You through?" he asked, suddenly getting that distant laughing-at-themselves view that always brought them into equilibrium.

"I guess I am."

"So how come you get to live the way it's right for you, and I don't get to have a dog?"

"Good grief," Annie said.

The sun went down while they were asking about the puppy. Not a real sunset, but a sudden cannonball dropping behind a mountain, jarring everything from gold to blue. They had six houses left on the route when the man answering the door said, "I don't think you deliver there, but you might try the house behind us, over on the next block. I thought I heard a new puppy being lonesome over there last night."

Stowe and Annie gave each other solemn looks. Reluctantly Stowe set the puppy down on his big clumsy feet. They coaxed him slowly around the block, urging him past the bulletin-board bushes he wanted to read with his nose.

Two young girls stopped circling their bikes in the street and began to pedal toward them, yelling a word.

The puppy squatted on his haunches and watched them

come. As they braked to a stop he rose wagging and gave them the same enthusiastic greeting he had given Stowe. "Teeny!" the younger one squealed. "Where've you been? Bad dog!" She yanked him up by the front legs.

"Hey!" Stowe exclaimed. He clamped his mouth shut.

"Gently," Annie said.

Stowe stared off over their heads, pretending not to see the puppy bestowing his kisses again out of an endless supply. He hated the puppy and the little girls, and himself for not being glad they were reunited. He glanced at Annie with one last surge of hope, but she slowly untied the bandanna and coiled the twine.

He whirled around and walked away. Teeny. For a dog name, it sucked.

He felt black and blue from the fall his life had taken since that morning's high at the bank. He ached for the puppy, but it was more than that. It was for everything he couldn't have, or had to give up, or would have to wait for. Always what he wanted belonged to somebody else, like Teeny, or used to, like his bike. Everything he had was secondhand or messed up by somebody careless, so he never got it shiny-new to polish and be proud of.

Even that damn hundred dollars on his wall. Without a word from Annie he felt it wasn't his. It ought to go for the extra rent. Or a trip to Maydell, Oklahoma. Or at least a phone call to find out if his grandfather was going to die and stop sending them money.

He looked at the sky. *I didn't mean that*, he said. *I'm just sad.*

He could hear Annie's old sandals flapping behind him,

making the only sound on the quiet street. The smells of supper changed from house to house as they passed: the run-over juice of a cherry pie, then pizza, then a fragrance so rare he had almost forgotten it. Steak. They walked a long time without speaking.

She caught up with him and glanced into his face. "Mad at me?" she asked.

He shrugged. They cut through the playground again.

Instead of detouring for the slide, Annie went right up the steps and down the slick slope. He stared at her, and slowly followed. Cool evening air rushed against his face. She stopped at the seesaws, smiling. They got on opposite sides, their weight balancing finally after the years of being unequal. Last winter, he remembered, she had been able to wear the flannel shirts and hiking boots he had outgrown.

"Hey," she said in her game-playing voice. "Tell me more about that piece of land. With the trees and the elephant."

They went up and down with the slow groaning sounds of a ship in a storm. He felt self-conscious.

"Tell me about the rabbits, George," she said earnestly.

"What?"

"Steinbeck. *Of Mice and Men*. It's about two drifters who wanted a little farm. Lennie's more brawn than brain. Someone's always doing a take-off on him. Duh, did I do somethin' wrong, George, did I, huh?"

"Oh, yeah," he said. He listened to the lonesome clink of a tetherball chain somewhere in the dusk of the playground. "Well, maybe rabbits. But mostly a dog. With puppies. Maybe a cat, too. Maybe even a horse."

68

"I would like a horse, too, George," she said with a soft slurred Lennie-voice.

"And a little house with all solar stuff. With a fireplace. So we could eat in front of it. And a great big kind of room with tools. For building things. A table saw. And all kinds of drawers full of screws and nails and cotter keys."

"And a potter's wheel?" Annie asked. "Could I? And a kiln? And a loom. And quilting frames I don't have to prop up on chairs." They were seesawing a little faster, shoving hard when their feet touched the ground. "And wrenches to keep your fancy motorcycles and cars and snowmobiles and whatever else running."

"Sure, tools for my chainsaw and my air compressor and the washing machine and the plumbing — I could keep it all repaired." He began to fly off the seat an inch or two each time her end of the seesaw hit the ground. "And we need fruit trees. Peaches and apples and pears and cherries."

"And strawberries and raspberries. I used to pick them wild up at Sutherland's Camp. I had never tasted raspberries till then. Every summer my mother made a little jar of jam to take back to Oklahoma. We would open it at Christmas and remember the mountains."

They went slower. "Sure, we'll have lots of raspberries. All you want." Far off on the basketball court someone was still shooting baskets in the twilight. *Plip. Plip.* Positioning himself. Testing. Then the shot. "Hey," he said softly, as if he had just thought of it, "how about if we buy Sutherland's Camp? And build us a house up there. And you can have jam all the time?"

"Oh, I would like that, George. I really would. How, George, how?"

He wished she made it easier to tell if she were serious or teasing. "I'm going to win a hundred thousand dollars in a contest. Or a sweepstakes thing that gives a boat, but we can sell the boat."

"Duh, George, I'm not sure people ever get something for nothing, do they, George?"

"It's not nothing. I send in every contest blank I see." Couldn't faith count for something? he wanted to ask. Didn't trying and hoping and believing and never-giving-up count? "Even the ones you put in the trash. I'll have to win someday, just from the law of averages."

They stood up and eased off the seesaw. One end dropped with a final groan. "I haven't given you much," Annie said. They started home across the baseball diamond. "I'm sorry. I wanted you to understand about integrity and kindness and responsibility and all those things, but I hope I haven't pushed you too hard. Has it been a reasonably normal childhood, do you think?"

"How do I know?" he said. "Normal is different for everybody."

She tripped over third base, and held his arm a moment. "You've always made me proud, Stowe. I know it hasn't been easy. Just us. I was trying very hard to show everybody I could bring you up just fine without help. Even give you some of the so-called advantages. I'm sorry the advantages never turned out to be skiing lessons or braces or new bikes."

They crossed a vacant lot and turned into their own street. Horseless was asleep at the curb, far up at the end of the block. "It's okay," he said. He didn't know what would reassure her. "I've liked it. Really." He sounded more brawn than brain, like Lennie.

Something flashed past them. They bumped together, startled, before they saw it was a beagle scuttling ahead of a jogger. For just a second, before he knew, Stowe thought it might be Teeny, choosing them.

Teeny. The stupidest name for a dog he ever heard of. If it had been his dog he would have named it Bill, after another wanderer who couldn't stay where he belonged. His father.

# ⇒ Four ⇐

Karla should have been waiting at dawn Saturday, knee-deep in cookies, when they rushed back from delivering papers. Stowe and Brownie crossed the street and tapped on her window, but the shade was drawn. They had to go to the door and knock. Mrs. McWhitty came weaving onto the porch, trying to get her arms into her robe.

"I thought Karla told you last night," she said.

They looked hopefully past her into the kitchen.

"She's backed out, fellows. She got a phone call last night that changed her mind."

"But she promised," Brownie said, trying to see cookies on a counter somewhere.

"Well, she's getting a lot of attention from that boy." Mrs. McWhitty felt to see if her hair looked funny. "I really am sorry. I thought it was cute of you two to ask her. She treats her grandparents the same way. They invite her for things and she backs out."

"Well," Stowe said, struggling to be polite, "we're sorry you got up."

"Yeah," Brownie said. "We ought to just have aimed a couple of bottle rockets through her window. She was already pushing her luck after that go-cart ride. Now it's war." He hesitated. "If it's all right with you, I mean."

Mrs. McWhitty laughed, looking like Karla's little sister. "Oh, I'm on your side. A lesson in manners would do her a lot of good."

"Tar and feathers at thirty paces?" Brownie asked, certain at last that the cookies weren't coming either.

She thought about it. "Maybe a squirt-can of shaving cream in the yard so we can just hose her down afterward?"

Annie laughed, too, when she heard, and gave them a bag of marshmallows to take for dessert. They filled the back of the pickup with boxes of food, a thermos jug, blankets, and a watermelon. Stowe added a box of scrap lumber for a campfire, and they were off.

"She practically invited us to declare war on Karla," he told Annie. "Like she was pretty well pissed off herself."

"Well, growing up fast, like Karla's doing, is hard on everybody," Annie said. "With the arms and legs getting ahead of the head. And the torso getting more so."

"Yeah, really," Brownie said glumly, cradling the marshmallows in his lap. Stowe watched the scenery, wondering for the first time in his life what Karla had looked like, asleep behind the drawn shade.

They went rattling up the cool dim canyon, along the creek that rattled down. Ahead of them the peaks were already in sunlight, crowded with the bronze spears of spruce forests.

"A squirt-can of something wouldn't be bad," Stowe

73

mused. "Remember when she got us with the whipped cream?"

"Oh, pathetic—we didn't get even for that yet," Brownie said. "Boy, this could turn out to be World War Three."

"Or the end of a beautiful friendship," Annie said.

"She shouldn't just get away with anything she wants to do," Stowe said. "You don't just blow off an invitation because a better one came along. And she's not about to help patch the go-cart up."

"I can get feathers," Brownie said. "What's like tar only it can wash off?"

"You sure you want it to wash off?" Stowe asked. "Syrup. Glue. Ketchup."

"Gross. Somebody would think she's bleeding and call an ambulance."

"The glue ought to go in her hair spray," Stowe said.

"Tell her we have a new kind of mud pack for her face," Brownie said. "Don't tell her it's cement."

"Hey," Annie said, "there's a lot of things in Karla's life she can't do anything about. Her face she can change. So let her."

Stowe said, "But the trouble is, she puts so much stuff on it, we're not sure she's still under there."

"So she comes up with a funny face occasionally. What about your walls?"

"You got funny walls?" Brownie asked.

"He's papering his room with fake money," Annie said. "When Karla saw that hundred-dollar bill, she asked if she could tear off five dollars' worth till next allowance."

"When was that?" Stowe asked uneasily.

74

"The day she spent all her money on fake fingernails."

Brownie said, "I'll bet the Kawasaki King takes half her allowance for gas, and wear and tear on the sissy bar."

"You two wouldn't be a little deflated at being dumped today for a motorcycle, would you?" Annie asked, trying not to smile.

"Miss Prissy Topheavy is the one that needs deflating," Stowe said. "We would've showed her a good time."

"Yeah, pull those little gold doodads out of her ears and give her a slow leak," Brownie said. "That'll bring her down to size."

They turned off the main road and curled through the draws and gulches of mountains that had looked like solid walls from a distance. They sampled the marshmallows. The sun was high enough to make a picket fence of shadows across the road as they skirted a stand of lodgepole pines.

They were getting close. Stowe watched Annie's face change. She seemed to lean forward, and the weekday strain turned loose of the corners of her mouth. The road got steep and rocky, and Horseless clanked along, its shocks mushing at every jolt.

"Look over there," Annie said, lifting a finger from the steering wheel to point. Off across a valley a train slowly threaded through a tunnel on the mountainside. Stowe watched as it curved in slow motion, too far away to wave at, and slid behind a cliff. It awed him, something so big, dwarfed against something so much bigger.

They curved, too, around a fold of hills, and saw the little sloping meadow of Sutherland's Camp fenced with dark pines. At its foot, the stream was slowed by old abandoned beaver dams into one golden pond after another.

"Look at that," Brownie said, impressed. "And they did it without any plastic or rocks."

Annie stopped Horseless under a pine tree. "Space. Look at all that beautiful space. You want to practice driving?"

Stowe looked nervously at Brownie. Brownie said, "My folks won't let me till I take Driver's Ed."

Annie's eyes questioned Stowe. "When I was your age I tried to wheedle everybody into letting me practice."

He wished she wouldn't push him. He was as interested in mechanical things as she was. But he just wasn't ready yet. He was sure he'd mash the gas pedal when he was supposed to mash the brake, and end up with the engine in the seat with him. He kicked the transmission hump with his heel. "Who wants to practice on this old clunker?"

He nudged Brownie out, and took the scraps of lumber to a jumble of rocks by the stream. Before Annie got the boxes set out, he had started a fire with only one match. They stood around it, reaching for its warmth in the morning chill. Then he and Annie fried sausages and eggs while the buttered bread toasted. Brownie watched, as silent and absorbed as they were. They heaped their tin plates and sat on rocks, hunting flat spots to set their cups of milk on.

"Wow," Brownie said. "This is *food*."

Annie asked, "Do your folks get up into the mountains much?"

Brownie dipped more eggs. "Well, when they got Terri and Sherri off to college, they kind of reverted to a second honeymoon, and it's been going on for a year or two. So when they get a vacation, they go to Vegas and have room service." He speared a sausage. "I'm not sure they remember me."

Annie lifted her face to the zigzag meeting of mountains and sky, smiling sadly.

"We don't get along that good," Brownie said unexpectedly. "I mean like you and Stowe. Like, I was watching you cook together."

Her smile got sadder. Stowe punched Brownie's shoulder. "Let's go see the beaver dams close up."

They jogged down through the aspen stumps that had been gnawed to points. At the first logjam holding back the dark still water Brownie rubbed a scab on his knuckle. "I guess nobody told *them* they had to take it all down."

They looked back at camp where Annie was putting tin plates back into boxes. "Up there is where the lodge used to be," Stowe said. "When she was little she promised herself she'd keep coming back here, no matter what happened to her. Because this was her favorite spot in the world."

"Do her folks know it's gone? Do they ever come back?"

"Well," Stowe said, not sure how much he wanted to tell, "there's just her dad back in Oklahoma. Her mother and brother died." He looked into Brownie's round, unjudging face. He had to talk to somebody, and it seemed easier after Brownie had opened up so unexpectedly to Annie to share himself in return. "Well, I mean there's other relatives left. Back in Maydell. It's crazy. One of them called me. He said my grandfather wanted to see me."

"See you?" Brownie laughed. "I thought he hated your guts."

"Well, I thought he did too. I mean, my mom and him — he told her just not to ever come back. So we've never even seen each other."

"So what started all that?"

Stowe hesitated. Then, as if a dam in him had shifted, the held-back words began to trickle. "I think he didn't like my dad. It happened about then, when she went off with him. I figured he wouldn't knock himself out liking me, either. But what's really weird, he sends my mom this little check every month. Like to help us out. And every month she writes back a thank-you letter just like they were perfectly friendly, and says how I'm growing and what I do in school and all that."

"Boy, I thought I was the only one with a weird family," Brownie said. "Where's your dad?"

Stowe jumped for a grass hummock and sank to his ankles in marsh mud. He wanted to talk about the phone call, but Brownie wasn't helping. "One of my mom's friends said he had a boat. I think his folks retired down in Mexico, so maybe he lives down that way, too, when he's not on his boat somewhere."

"Hey, a boat would be neat. Why don't you live with him?"

Annie had cleared camp and was walking slowly across

the meadow. "I don't know," Stowe said warily, watching her. "He has girl friends and stuff. Anyway, I like it here too much. I like mountains."

"Yeah, but don't you want to know more about him than that?"

He tried to decide. What did he know about a man named Bill Garrett? It was the name he put on the forms he had to fill out in school. Address? Blank. Occupation? Blank. Does he remember you or think of you? Blank. But what did he know? He tried to grope back to his first memories. It had been uncomfortable, like visiting some-one, when his dad came home. He remembered cigarette smoke and the toilet seat up and voices shouting in the other room when he woke in the night. And their faces, afterwards, like those almost-real Halloween masks with real eyes looking through.

"I guess I don't really want to know about him," he said. "This way I can imagine him any way I want to." How could you miss what you didn't have? He tried to think how he would imagine him if he wanted to. A blankness filled his mind. "He was gone a lot." He tried to explain it the way Annie had explained it to him. "Some people just don't want to be around kids much. They get nervous. It's just the way they are."

"But don't you even hear from him? Like Christmas?"

Stowe pranced briskly to warm the water squishing in his sneakers. "Well, he moves around, and we moved around different places, till we came here. So we kind of lost each other. I guess if he wanted to find us he could." There was an address. Annie had told him. She kept it with her, for emergencies, a little piece of Bill Garrett he had never asked to know.

"Weird," Brownie said. "But maybe you've got it easier. With just one parent."

Stowe began to run. "You think so?" he yelled back. He leaped aspen logs that the beavers had felled and found too heavy to sluice down to the ponds. Didn't Brownie remember the day he came over and caught him trying to soothe his scraped, raw face, and said, Were you shaving with a razor? You're supposed to use *lather*, dummy. Did he think all that part was easy? Annie never used lather on her legs. He lived in dread of making mistakes like that, doing girl-things. Couldn't Brownie tell?

Brownie jogged patiently behind him. "Well, anyway, if you're going to stay with just your mom, you're lucky she's not all bitchy and pitiful from thinking she has it tough."

Stowe slowed to a walk, and hunted her through the trees. She had climbed to the top of the meadow. All at once she dropped to her knees and rolled down the slope like a shotgunned rustler in some old TV rerun. Brownie's mouth flipped open in a startled smile. They watched her stand up dizzily and pick the weeds out of her hair.

"Weird," Brownie giggled.

Annie saw them and waved. She came toward them, shaking one leg occasionally in a Charlie Chaplin walk to get the twigs out of her jeans. Stowe felt a jolt of gladness. Please, his heart said. Let me be better to her than they were.

"Don't she have any boy friends?" Brownie asked.

Stowe hesitated, not wanting to make her seem more

weird than she already seemed by saying no. "Sure." He made a laugh. "Us."

After lunch they were so full of hamburgers they rocked up the watermelon in the creek to cool for midafternoon. They moved the blankets into the whispery shade of a pine, and sprawled out, smelling cozily of onion and mustard. The sky was the too-perfect blue of a travel poster through Stowe's lashes. The clouds hung like eagles over the distant peaks. Happy, he thought. This is happy.

Annie's head bobbed back and forth between her library book on wildflowers and the real thing growing at the edge of her blanket. Brownie said, "Yuck, that reminds me. I've got to read a book."

"In the summer?" Stowe asked. Annie gave them both a lifted-eyebrow look, and went back to her flowers.

"Summer's the reason," Brownie said. "My folks made me join this stupid reading-club thing, to keep me out of trouble this last month. You have to read a book a week, at least. And then write a thing about it. It's worse than school."

"How many have you read?"

"One about Dracula. It was pretty neat. Now I'm reading one about Alferd Packer."

"Who's Alfred—"

"Alferd."

"Who's Alferd Packer?"

"He was this guy that got snowbound up in the mountains with these other guys. So he ate them."

"Gross. What for?"

"So he wouldn't starve, dumbdumb."

Annie said, "A long time ago, people ate their captives so they could, you know, get their bravery and strength. But being civilized, Alferd might have had in mind gold watches."

"Why didn't he eat their watches, then?" Stowe asked.

"And go tick tick tick the rest of his days?" Brownie asked.

They made little chuckles of contentment and laziness. Annie said, "Coo, what a decision. Could I eat someone, to keep myself alive?"

"Well, if somebody just froze or something, you might as well get the good out of them," Brownie said drowsily.

Stowe said, "But not just kill them off for munchies."

They lay still, studying the Japanese shapes of the pine branches against the sky. Big black flies came at them like fighter planes, their engines revved to a whine. Stowe tried to imagine what the meadow had looked like thirty years before. The little log cabins. The dining-room smells. The tiny seedling that had become the tree he was looking up through.

"Did they have thick walls?" he asked, thinking of the rooms Annie had slept and eaten in, when she was young. Before they all disappeared, like someone dying.

Annie followed his gaze. "Here? Oh, windowsills two feet deep. It was a wonderful grubby old place, full of history. Somebody's old ranch originally, I think. Or a stage stop."

"What did your brother do?" It seemed important to know the beginnings that had led crookedly through the years to the phone call he couldn't tell her about.

82

"He was a baby, those years. Seven years younger than I was. He stayed close to my mother. She wasn't well, even then, so my father and I . . . " She smiled and pointed to Brownie, who had gone to sleep. In a softer voice she said, "We did everything together. Fished. Hiked. Helped the wrangler with the horses. All those years when I was the only child, he and I . . ." She picked a tiny stem of bedstraw and held it to Stowe's nose. It smelled like honey. "Those were good times." She got up and pushed the little flower into a buttonhole of her shirt. "Then Chris got old enough to do those things with him."

"Why didn't all three of you do things?"

She thought back. "Well, someone had to stay with my mother more. And—I don't know. My father loved the idea of a son. Before Chris came, I was the substitute son. Then he had the living, breathing, real thing."

Stowe followed her toward a grove of young trees that had taken root around an old foundation stone. "And then my grandmother died?" It sounded strange. Actually she hadn't been his grandmother. He came too late.

"She was sick a long time. I sort of turned into the mother. You know, making the same hot meals and pressing the permanent-press shirts because she had." She made a mock laugh. "Can you believe I kept books? Your grandfather and great-uncle Otis had a welding shop. They still do, as a matter of fact. I worked there—my figures never came out right. I hated it. Hated being courted by nice dumb little-town boys who proposed during half-time at football games."

"Why didn't you pack up and go somewhere better?" Stowe asked. He guessed she had told him all this before, when he was little, or thought he knew, somehow, because she did.

"I almost had enough money — or maybe it was courage — to leave. Your father saved me from deciding if I was ready or not."

"How?"

"By stopping off in Maydell on his way to fame and fortune. Actually he had just been fired from a public relations job with a traveling rock group. But to me he was Mr. Culture coming to rescue me from stagnation and dust devils." She smiled at Stowe. "And sinfully handsome he was. That level look you get sometimes when you're going to shake the world till it rattles."

"Did he ask you at a football game?"

Her face went soft with distance. "He climbed through my bedroom window like in a comic opera and asked me. And I said, Yes, oh, yes — thank you! because I was so grateful to be rescued. Even if I was just somebody innocent he could have fun shaping." She thought about it, and shrugged. "Being innocent and shapeless when you're twenty-seven helps you make quick decisions."

"Was that when your dad stopped liking you?" Stowe pushed back a squawbush and stepped across a thick flagstone that must have been the threshold of a house. "When did that happen?"

"When I left." Annie hesitated, and followed him through the imaginary door. "His life changed. He had taken for granted I would always be there, washing his socks and keeping his books."

Stowe said uncertainly, "I wasn't sure. I thought — maybe it was me. Me he didn't like."

"Oh, Stowe," she said in dismay. "No. It was because of Chris. I told you all that."

"All what?"

"Oh, child." She pushed back her straggling hair. "Your uncle Chris." She felt the strangeness of the word, too, because he hadn't lived to be his uncle Chris. "Your grandfather loved him more than anything in the world. You have to understand that. When I left with your father, Chris was all he had left of his family. You see?"

Because it seemed so important to her, he nodded.

"When your father and I decided to get married, out in Phoenix, my dad wouldn't come. But Chris came. And just outside of Phoenix — I've told you, Stowe."

She looked so sad and taut that he longed to help her. "Was that when he got killed?"

"It was like I had done it. Because he was coming to my wedding. Then, when I went home for the funeral, that was when your grandfather . . ."

Stowe waited, giving her time.

"He sent word by Aunt Fritzi that he didn't want to see me. Ever. He said I had destroyed his family." She suddenly slung tears off her cheeks. "Why did he say that? I was his family!" She began to walk, faster and faster, toward the creek. Stowe followed, trying to see what she saw through the bitter dust of the years. But when he caught up with her she said, "I didn't mean that. You have to understand how much he'd lost, and how empty his life suddenly was."

"He could have filled it up with us," he said.

"I know." Down in the stream's shadowy current a grey

trout rested. "I would like to go visit him, Stowe. It hurts me. It hurts me not to try to reconcile."

He stared at the quivering water, growing as cold as the wet stones. He couldn't believe she meant it. She hadn't even dared to call.

"Why?" he asked, too sharply. "That would be crazy. Leave him alone — he picked the way he wanted to live." He clamped his mouth shut, surprised at himself. But he couldn't let a man like that come between them after all they'd gone through, all those us-against-the-world years.

"But, Stowe, if something should happen." She made a quick twitch of smile to show how unlikely dying was. "And I hadn't tried to see him, or tell him or show him . . ."

Don't push me, he begged her in his mind. Please just stay out of it. He's not going to die — he's going to live and mess up our lives and I can't ask you what I ought to do!

He said, "Wouldn't it be simpler just to go on hating him?"

"I don't hate him, Stowe. I don't want you to hate him, either. It's such a waste."

"I do, though," he said.

Her face squeezed up with pain. "That's because you don't have the good times to remember. You don't understand how much joy and love he's missed. Try to, when you're older."

"Sure," he said, stiff-mouthed. "Maybe I can understand Mr. Culture, too, someday, like you do your dad."

She put her hands over her face and rubbed her closed eyes.

"I'm sorry," he said. He felt like the twisted roots at his feet that dangled out into space above the eroded bank.

"No, it's all right." She looked tired.

"But let things stay the way they are. Can't you?"

She reached out shyly and picked the dried seed pods that had stuck to his shirt sleeve. With an effort she lifted the corners of her mouth. "I'll bet there's something you didn't realize. When I went back to the funeral, my dad had already told Aunt Fritzi to get rid of all Chris's things, or he'd burn them. She asked me if I wanted Chris's old pickup."

Stowe blinked. "You mean — was that Horseless?"

"Horseless. I drove it back to Phoenix. I needed Horseless. Your father always had the car. He was on the road most of the time. He had already discovered a young singer. He was going to be her manager. So I needed Horseless."

Stowe turned around with her to look at the battered old truck slumped beside the campfire rocks.

"You and Horseless have come a long way together," Annie said. "In all those places — the one constant thing in our lives. Our little home-away-from-home, carrying us where we had to go."

He nodded, trying to understand. Those days, he had never questioned or judged or compared it with other cars. Not until they came to live in a resort town where Corvettes and Jeeps with chrome roll-bars leaped ahead at stop lights and left him hot-faced and full of longings. It seemed dumb, now. "Old clunker," he said wonderingly.

A sound edged between them. They turned. "Where's everybody?" Brownie yelled from the pine tree. He came out, wagging with puppy looseness, and jolted down the slope toward them. "Is it time for watermelon yet?"

Stowe held the shattered closeness a second, and let it drop the way Annie had dropped Horseless's broken mirror. He yelled, "Sure, get it out of the refrigerator."

Halfway up the slope he turned back to see why Annie wasn't following. She had stopped dead still at a small bush. "Oh, Stowe," she called, with a little-girl face. "Raspberries!"

While they were gnawing melon slices like a band of harmonica players, Brownie said, "Where's this old mine where we were going to ditch Karla?"

Stowe frowned. He had more or less planned to wander off and show it to Brownie without saying anything about it. He wished Brownie had more practice keeping his mouth shut, the kind of practice people got from having mothers who liked all the same things they did. He made his face look uninterested. "Wouldn't be much fun without Karla squealing."

"I'd still like to see it," Brownie said, not helping a bit.

"Me, too," Annie said brightly. "We didn't really get to explore it that first time. Did you bring a flashlight?"

Stowe flicked an anxious glance at Brownie. Was he thinking she would spoil their fun, inviting herself along like that? And even worse, did Brownie expect him to do something about it? He said carefully, "Did we bring one?"

"Yeah, we brought it," Brownie said. "But, Stowe, we ought to make torches, instead, like in the movies."

"Probably not," Annie said, helping them put melon rinds in a sack to take home. "Could blow ourselves up if we hit a pocket of methane." Stowe checked Brownie's face again. He had stopped to listen, round-eyed. "Unless we've already stepped on an old, unstable stick of dynamite somebody left behind when they stopped working the mine." She grinned in anticipation.

Stowe hung undecided. He certainly didn't want Brownie to think his mother went along all the time to take care of him. On the other hand, he realized she had just made it easier for him. He cleared his throat experimentally. "You want to come with us?"

"Yeah," Brownie agreed hurriedly. "So you can get blown up, too?"

"Thought you'd never ask," Annie said.

They climbed up through a long slope of trees and followed a narrow overgrown road into a bushy draw. They all began to puff as the sun bore down on them. Suddenly Stowe veered off over a mound of yellowish rubble. "Here's the tailings," he called. Annie and Brownie climbed up after him. A jagged opening, like the mouth of a cave, was almost blocked by fallen rock.

"Hey," Brownie said, holding back. "Do we have to crawl?"

"Just past the cave-in," Stowe said. "Then it's big."

They stooped low and clambered over the sharp broken granite. Cool air enclosed them, damp and breathing. They could see little sparse green beards of moss on the rocks near the entrance. They went forward into dimness. Stowe switched on the flashlight. A long puddle of black water blocked their way. Drainage from the tunnel had backed up, stopped by the rockfall. Some earlier explorer had laid a log across two rocks to form a rickety bridge just clearing the water.

"Is it deep?" Brownie asked.

"Just a few inches," Stowe said. "But yucky." He eased across the sagging log and turned the light on it so Annie and Brownie could see where to step. Then he swung the light around to show them where they were going.

The tunnel had been blasted from solid rock. The floor was almost level, but strewn with rubble and crossed by little railroad ties moldering in seepage.

"You sure you know where this goes?" Brownie asked.

"Not really," Stowe said, interrupting Annie who started to say the same thing. "We just came in a little way last time, without a light." Like a tour guide, he showed them the arched stone roof. Iron oxide made dripping water on one wall look like a bleeding wound.

"Karla didn't know what she'd be missing," Brownie said hollowly, tripping over a tie. "What were the tracks for?"

"To bring out the ore in carts," Stowe said.

They crept along behind the wavering light. The tiny glow of the entrance disappeared. After the sunshine, the coldness and stillness seemed unreal. A side tunnel opened to their left, curving out of sight into blackness. Stowe faltered, then chose the way with less shadows.

Light hitting the rough walls made people-shapes appear and slide away. A coating that was not exactly mold or slime covered the rocks. They began to go for long stretches without speaking. The silence filled with the eerie sound of dripping water. Another tunnel wandered off to the right.

"Wait up," Annie called from behind them. She had lost her moccasin in a muddy spot. Stowe held the light's long beam on her while she found it and banged the silt off against the wall.

"Want to ditch her?" Brownie asked in a whisper. "Like we meant to with Karla?"

"Ditch her?" He stalled, trying to decide if Brownie was ticked off because she had come, or simply wanted a substitute for the game they had anticipated. He guessed he owed Brownie some fun for accepting Annie without any of the dumb comments he'd made the day they built the dam. "How?" he whispered back.

"Like this." Brownie pushed down on Stowe's thumb. The flashlight went out. Stowe felt a prickle of delight as its afterimage gave way to the first absolute darkness he had ever experienced.

"Hey," Annie said from a distance. "What happened?"

"Sh-hh," Brownie breathed. They stood motionless.

"Okay, you jokers. If you're planning to scare me, forget it. Anybody touches me gets whomped senseless with a wet moccasin."

They shook with silent giggles and waited.

"Well," Annie said finally. Her voice vibrated off into emptiness. "So long. If you don't find your way out by night, Horseless and I will just have to go home without you."

They waited, holding their breath. Stowe shivered with a mixture of pleasure and uneasiness. Annie was playing along, so far. It had all happened so suddenly he hadn't had time to consider how to end it. Turn the light back on and laugh? He wished he knew what Brownie had in mind.

Brownie very slowly leaned away. Stowe thought he heard him ease to the floor. So they were going to sit. Let her blunder-and-wonder for a while. Why not? It was all in fun. But only a few minutes. He remembered the side tunnels curving off. When her voice came from far enough away he would switch on the light and laugh.

They waited. Stowe held his breath to listen. Water dripped somewhere. If she were groping her way along the tunnel wall they should hear an occasional footstep, a tiny grinding of loose rock. He felt out for Brownie. All he felt was cold air.

He turned in a small panic, and banged his head against the jagged wall. The flashlight flew out of his hand. It hit something hard, bounced, and rolled away with a metallic jiggle.

Stowe knelt and groped. He and Brownie bumped heads. The utter darkness smothered him. He felt along the wet floor with a hand that hardly seemed to be there. He could hear Brownie's breath rasping as he groped along the other wall.

"Brownie," he whispered.

"Sh-h."

"But, Brownie, where's the stupid flashlight?"

"I don't know — hunt!" Brownie whispered.

They crawled along, shoulder to shoulder, making anxious sweeps with their hands.

"Where'd your mom go?" Brownie asked in Stowe's ear.

"Did you hear steps? I didn't."

"Then what's she doing? Just standing somewhere?"

They strained to see in the blackness. A hand suddenly poked Stowe in the nose. He yelped.

"Sh-h," Brownie ordered. "I didn't mean to hit you. I was just seeing if I could see my hand before my face."

"Well, see if you can keep it out of *my* face," Stowe said, forgetting to whisper.

"How am I going to know where your face is?"

"Find the flashlight, stupid." They crawled through a trickle of water.

"Stowe, it couldn't have rolled this far. Let's turn around." They felt for a wall. Stowe's hand swept cold air. He took two steps on his soggy knees. Nothing. Blackness.

"Oh, wow," Brownie said beside him. "Where's the wall?"

"Maybe we're at a tunnel that forks off."

"That was way back there."

"Then — maybe it's another tunnel we were just coming to when we turned off the light."

"Oh jeez, oh jeez," Brownie said. He caught the back of Stowe's shirt. "Let's stick together, Stowe. Let's hold hands."

They groped until their fingers meshed. Then they couldn't crawl forward on their hands — they were three-pronged like a sack race. "This is stupid," Stowe said. He took a deep breath. "Mom!" he called with all his might.

The sound went ringing off. In the silence the great mass above them seemed to shift heavily. Fear came out in goosebumps on Stowe's arms. They had the whole weight of a mountain over their heads. How much vibration did it take to bring all those tons of rock tumbling down? Or did they ever just get tired and turn loose?

"She's already out." Brownie shivered. "She's gone."

"You sure?" It didn't seem right. He couldn't remember a time when he had called and she didn't answer. Would she leave them there with all that methane stuff and leftover dynamite? "Maybe she went the wrong way and got lost."

Brownie scrabbled at something in the rocks. "I've found it!" Stowe heard a click as he switched the flashlight on. Nothing happened. Batteries rattled as Brownie shook the flashlight and pounded it against his hand.

"What's the matter?"

"Won't come on," Brownie said anxiously, shaking it again. Stowe groped for it, and tightened everything that screwed. He clicked the switch. Nothing.

Annie's voice beside them asked, "What happened?"

They both screeched as if she had suddenly breathed dragon fire, and banged into each other, startled by her nearness.

"Where were you?" Stowe exclaimed. "You didn't answer!"

Annie said, "Really? I thought we were playing jokes. Besides, I yelled for you first, remember. And *you* didn't answer. What's wrong with the flashlight?"

Stowe clicked it again. "The bulb broke, or something."

Annie found his hand and took the flashlight. They listened as she slid out the batteries and put them back a different way. One fell. They all gasped and knelt to hunt it, jerking back as they grabbed each other's fingers by

94

mistake. Annie found it. They heard the switch click. Nothing.

"Oh jeez," Brownie murmured.

Stowe felt apprehension like a cold breath on the back of his neck. He stood up and revolved slowly. "So which way do we go?" he asked, making his voice ordinary.

"You mean you two intrepid jokers are lost?" Annie said. She had arranged her voice as carefully as his.

"Well, personally I am," Brownie gulped.

Stowe reached out and touched a damp wall. He had no idea which way led out and which would lead them farther into the black depths of the mine. Tiny shivers began to trill through him.

Annie said, "Now wait a minute — wait a minute." She found them both and took their arms. "Hold still. We have to think."

"Oh, God, we *are* lost then," Brownie said.

"Not really, we're still where we were before," Stowe said evenly. "We just don't know which way is out." He thought what that meant, and prickled with fear.

"Now wait," Annie said. He heard a little panicky wiggle in her voice. "There's got to be some way of knowing. Think."

"I'm thinking," Brownie said. "I'm thinking who knows to look for us at Motherland Camp?"

"Sutherland," Stowe said.

"Smotherland, motherland, who's going to look for us in here?"

"The track," Annie said. "Wouldn't the track slope down all the way to the entrance?"

Stowe drew a calming breath and put his mind in gear.

95

"Maybe not, if a horse or one of those winch things pulled it. Anyway, we still couldn't tell which way the tracks sloped."

They listened to each other's breathing. Somewhere in what she had said was something usable, Stowe knew. But what? He had to grasp it. The mine had been his idea, and he had dropped the flashlight. He strained against his fear. Tracks. Downhill.

"The water," he said.

Annie groaned. "Of course."

"What about the water?" Brownie asked, but they were already on their knees, patting the floor. He came toppling down beside them. "What do you mean, the water?"

"They had to dig the tunnel so it would drain," Stowe said. "Find a trickle."

Brownie's bewildered fingers poked him in the face again. "Find a what?"

Stowe splatted water. "Never mind!" He had a trickle. He dropped the edge of his hand across it in a light karate chop and waited. Annie and Brownie froze, holding their breath. For long seconds all he could feel was wetness. He poked a finger on either side of the little dam his rigid hand had made, feeling silty water. Then he slowly tensed. He could feel it. A difference. Water was gathering against the back of his hand. And when he poked in front of his palm there was only silt.

He shivered in thankfulness and strained closer, listening, feeling. He had to be sure. Suddenly he lifted his hand and heard the trickle start again, draining the tiny pool that had collected behind his hand. He stood up, jubilant, and slid his fingers along the wall. "It's this way," he said, and started off in the direction the trickle had taken.

He felt Annie fumble for his shoulder and pat it in silent pride.

She said, "Let's walk abreast, so we can feel both walls. If we go along just one wall we could follow a curve right around into a side tunnel without knowing it."

They took hands and started slowly through the blackness.

"Jeez, are you sure about this?" Brownie asked, stumbling along between them.

Stowe gulped. Had he done it right?

Annie said, "Let's trust him. Trickle, Brownie."

They lurched on, sliding their palms along the broken granite, too intent to talk. It had to be the right direction. She had let him do it. She hadn't even dammed the water herself to double-check.

"We could sing," Annie said. " 'Oh, the moon shines tonight on pretty Redwing —' " There was black silence. No one knew the next line.

"You know any longer ones?" Brownie murmured between them. They both burst out laughing at the same moment.

Far ahead, the curve of the tunnel shifted gently, and they saw the dim miraculous glow of the entrance. They blundered toward it, cheering. It grew. They could see the world out there, glowing like a furnace. Stowe gave a joyful yelp and led them forward.

As they teetered single-file across the log bridge, Annie's wet moccasins slipped out from under her. She plopped into the drainage pool up to her shins. Stowe reached past Brownie to catch her hand, but the log rolled off its rock props and he and Brownie went splashing in beside her. Their relief exploded into groans and whoops as they sloshed toward the light. Annie stopped and did a little dance in the water. "Wait-wait. Lost a moccasin again."

They all felt among the sunken rocks and rotting unknowns with their feet, making exaggerated groans of disgust. Stowe brought it up, hooked to the slimy toe of his sneaker.

"Mom. You're weird."

"Yeah, Mom." Suddenly Brownie cackled, "Wow, listen to me — I'm saying Yeah Mom just like Stowe. Sorry."

"She doesn't mind," Stowe said. "Yetta and Tyler do it all the time. But I'm the only one that gets to say she's weird."

They crawled out of the mouth of the tunnel and stood in the sunshine. They looked at each other with huge grins, and wrung out the legs of their jeans. Annie laughed, "If you think I'm weird, imagine getting lost in there with Karla."

"Jeez," Brownie said solemnly. "Really."

When they saw Horseless, they began to run, starved.

While the pork and beans were heating they dried themselves at the fire and after supper they sat, warm and full, and watched the peaks turn black. The pines talked, relaying a message from far away, and the stream rushed downhill, murmuring like the White Rabbit, I'm late, I'm late . . .

Annie, murmuring too, asked, "You know what's a wonderful thing?" Stowe waited, thinking of answers. The sound of the stream. Her voice. Being safe and together. "Rising ground," she said. "Slopes. Hills. Places that promise you tops."

Stowe lifted his face. Night was slowly climbing out of the meadow where they sat toward the high, last rim of light. He nodded.

"Papers in the morning," she reminded them, saying it to the fire that had entranced them all.

"Not yet," Stowe begged. He could have hunched there all night, between his two favorite people, in his favorite little piece of the world, sated with adventure and happiness. He had decided where the house would be. On that very spot, where the tall trees framed a sawtoothed mountain and the stream slid with a final silver glint around the foot of the meadow. Its walls would be thick. Moss would grow on its roof, and it would last forever.

"Wow," Brownie said wistfully, "this has been a good day." They lingered until the fire sank to coals. They toasted the last three marshmallows. "It's so nice and peaceful it's almost a pity to go to war with Karla tomorrow."

Stowe made an uneasy laugh. He had hoped the war was just a funny idea to talk about and never get around to. He started to glance at Annie to see how she had reacted, but stopped. He was always doing that. He got up and wet the coals with a frying-pan of water from the stream, and began to load Horseless with the picnic things.

Before they had rounded their second curve, Brownie's

head slumped against the rattling window and he was asleep.

Stowe settled himself between them with his feet propped on the warm hump of Horseless's transmission. His eyes ached with the picnicky feeling of too much sun and wind and beauty.

He said softly, "That was dumb of us. Turning off the light in there."

Annie nodded. "The joke would have worked better if the flashlight had worked better."

He wished she could know it had been Brownie's idea, but it didn't seem fair to say so. He squirmed, stirring the campfire smell in his clothes. "Thanks for giving me the idea that water runs downhill."

Annie laughed. After a moment she said, "Thanks for letting me feel welcome."

He grew still, realizing she had known that her wanting to go with them had put him in a predicament. He watched Horseless's headlights trigger little cat's eyes on the road markers as they floated around the curves, and peace lulled him.

He was almost asleep himself when Annie said, "Maybe we'll have another letter from Aunt Fritzi when we get home. I hope so." He tensed, waiting for her to say she ought to call. Instead, she said, "Oh, Stowe, what am I going to do? If he's worse . . ."

"He's not. He's better." He caught his lip. "I mean, I just feel like he is."

"I hope so," she said. "I know going to see him might not work. It could even make things worse. And I know we don't have money for a trip like that. But just the same —" She sighed. "When this kind of thing happens, an illness or something unexpected, I feel like a grasshopper at the end of summer. Improvident."

"What's that?"

"As if I'd fiddled my life away instead of providing for the winter like all those industrious ants. I should have money for emergencies. Not just enough to get by." She dropped her hand on his knee. "I'm not taking good care of you. It scares me."

"You take care of me," he said. He brushed away the sudden picture of the hundred dollars taped to the wall of his room. He couldn't offer to share it if the first thing she'd want to do was take off for Maydell, Oklahoma, and more unhappiness. On the other hand, if something happened and she really really needed it, he'd naturally give it to her in a minute. His muscles turned loose at the decision. We take care of each other, he thought, letting his head bob to the chink-chink of the tailgate chains. Out loud he told her, "I'm glad we had grasshopper summers. Really."

Annie made a soft laugh. "Do you remember when we were driving that night, moving here, and I thought a car with just one headlight was coming toward us and I dimmed our lights? And the other light sort of blinked off and on again, and all at once this huge train roared by?"

Stowe chuckled. "I remember." His eyes felt cooler when he shut them. He thought of all the times they had rattled through the night to new places, lulled by the safe, steady heartthrobs of the engine. "Do you remember when I was little and I'd say, 'Mom, do we have plenty of gas?' and you'd say, 'Yes,' and I'd say, 'Do you know how to get there without me to read the signs?' and you'd say, 'Yes'? And I'd say, 'Then I guess I'll take a little nap.'"

"I remember," Annie said, and he felt the little rumble of her laugh as he slid to sleep against her shoulder.

# ➤ Five ◄

**B**rownie was folding papers when Stowe staggered out on the porch the next morning. Brownie grinned and held up a battered pillow. "Are you saying you spent the night?" Stowe mumbled, too sleepy to make sense of it.

"For the war, dumbdumb. Feathers."

Stowe began to stuff the funnies and advertizing supplements into his thick Sunday papers. He couldn't understand why Brownie was so eager, when it hadn't been his picnic Karla had brushed off, or even his go-cart she had totaled. But it looked as if they were really going to do it.

"What have you got, to stick feathers on with?" Brownie asked.

Stowe wet his lip. "I'm not sure we've got anything." He lifted his mouth into a coaxing smile. "Hey, why don't we just go sit on her lawn and kid her about the crazy stuff she used to do? About how it was."

"Oh, come on," Brownie said. "Mustard? Furniture polish? You've got something." He studied Stowe's face.

"Hey, what's the matter? She's expecting it. She'll love it."

"It's not Karla I'm thinking about." It was hard to explain.

"Who?"

Stowe looped his bag over the handlebars of his bike. "Well, mothers don't go for stuff like that." He handed Brownie the extra bag he used when he helped.

"Which mothers?" Brownie asked. "Karla's mom thinks it's a hot idea."

"Ours might not, though."

"Mine won't know about it," Brownie said. He waited in one of those silences that coiled Stowe like a spring. Finally he said, "So is she going to let you, or what?"

"I didn't ask her," Stowe said. "I don't ask her stuff like that." The simple fact was that he didn't have to. He knew how she reacted to most things. He knew this was a Think-about-it-carefully-Stowe situation and Brownie was forcing him to feel instead of think. "I can decide things for myself."

Brownie made a sour face. "Jeez, Stowe, don't you ever just do something crazy and then think later whether you should have or not?"

He caught Brownie's eyes and held them in a steady stare. "Yes." His throat tensed, but he said, "That phone call that came. I didn't tell her about that."

Brownie lifted his shoulders. "So okay. I can bring a can of shaving cream."

"I'll bring it," Stowe said.

"But I can just swipe it at home from my—"

"I know what you can do," Stowe exclaimed. "But I'll bring it, okay?"

Brownie made his puppy-dog smile. "If that's what turns you on." He rammed his pillow under his shirt and got on his bike, looking like Santa Claus about to goof up and deliver the toys in August.

"Hey, listen," Stowe said sharply, unable to let it stop there. "You keep acting like I need somebody to tell me everything I do."

"Me?" Brownie wheeled in a tight doughnut, waiting.

"Yeah! Like I need my mom's approval or have to check how she's reacting to everything. Well, I don't! There's a lot of stuff she never knows, that I just work out myself. Like that call about my grandfather. I didn't want to tell her about it. So I didn't. And I'm not going to, either."

He stopped, startled by what he'd heard himself say. But Brownie had come to a stop, too, interested.

He plunged on. "It would just make her feel worse. Besides, it was *my* call. So I get to say what I get to do about it. So why should I let an old sick man rearrange our lives?"

"Aren't you going to go see him like he wanted, either?"

"Why should I? All those things my mom's cousin thought he was telling him — he could have been mumbling around out of his head. I'd look stupid running out there to Oklahoma and finding out he didn't remember a thing he said."

Brownie grinned. "Or even if he'd meant it, he might take one look at you and change his mind."

"Right," Stowe said. He suddenly grinned, too,

warmed by the flicker of admiration he had caught in Brownie's eyes. "So as far as I'm concerned, she's better off not knowing. And that's it."

He jabbed at the kickstand of his bike like some kind of general spurring a black charger. He had just made the kind of crazy spontaneous decision he'd always wanted to make.

Brownie went home after breakfast to tackle Alferd Packer. Stowe threw himself down on his unmade bed and stared at Ben Franklin. He guessed he felt calm about his decision. Proud, even. All he had to do was hold back any anxiety about what might happen if Harold called again or Annie found out some other way, or whether he was holding back something she had the right to know. He tossed uneasily. For now he had to figure how to buy shaving cream when every cent he had was tied up in that little grey-green rectangle on the wall.

It was like him, he thought. Waiting there, all focused and full of power he didn't know how to use. He got up, tired already, and looked through his hiding places. He had cleaned them out. He went into the living room where Annie was shuffling big pieced squares of cloth on the floor, trying to get a quilt laid out in the right pattern. He watched her crawl through the bright colors, scraping her hair out of her eyes, and knew he couldn't ask her for money to fight Karla's war.

He went down the street to see if the corner man would let him mow the lawn two days early, but everybody was at church. He sighed, and pulled a plastic trash bag from his pocket. He went along the creek picking up aluminum cans and returnable bottles. In a little over an hour he had his sack full, and was two miles from home.

He turned his salvage in at the supermarket and chose the squirt can he wanted. At the check-out counter he wondered if everyone thought he was buying it for himself. He guessed he would be, sooner than he liked to think. People would expect him to do other things with it than squirt girls, and other things with girls than chase them with shaving cream.

That afternoon he helped Annie clean house and weed the garden. Partly because they had played off all day Saturday, and partly to earn some advance credit to balance out what he was planning. But mostly to repay somehow for what his reckless decision might have denied her. The shadows were already stretching when he saw Brownie peer in through the front screen.

He wished Annie had gone to the store or something. At least she was in the back yard, watering the bare spots in Sir Landlard's lawn. But that wasn't going to stop her from knowing the minute war was declared across the street. He signaled Brownie to stay out on the porch, and went to get the shaving cream from under his socks. In the kitchen a bottle of ketchup was the only sticky stuff he could find. He slipped quietly out with his contributions.

"All right!" Brownie beamed, and popped them into a big paper sack on the top step. A little feather puffed out as he folded the top down. "Ready?" he asked.

Stowe looked back into the house. He guessed he felt the way real soldiers did. What they were doing seemed weird, but they had said they would do it. And once they had decided to, things like pride and solidarity somehow took over where good sense left off. "Sure," he said.

They went over and knocked. Nobody answered. They looked around, wondering what to do. Stowe hated to suggest they go back over to his house and rebuild the go-cart, or anything as practical as that.

Brownie sat down impatiently on the top step. After a moment Stowe sat beside him. He felt self-conscious. They must look like store mannequins advertizing cutoff jeans and saggy T-shirts. Even without Karla there, he could feel himself growing artificial again, aware of the pose he held and the sunset light on his face. He hated feeling the constant little itch of anxiety over what to do and who to believe and how to get through the things he had to get through.

"She's probably off somewhere letting the Kawasaki King have a ride," Brownie said.

"What do you mean?" It sounded backward.

"You know."

"Oh." He tried not to look shocked. "Yeah, probably." He wished Brownie wouldn't get off on stuff like that, imagining things. Actually it told him more about Brownie than it did about Karla. "No, I don't think so," he said, regretting having agreed so easily.

He couldn't figure how Brownie always managed to sound so knowing, when he knew for a fact Brownie didn't understand half the things they looked up in his folks' encyclopedia of sex. Having boy-crazy twin sisters had helped, maybe. Who was he kidding — having crazy-for-each-other parents helped.

"That was a dumb thing to say," he told Brownie.

"You think so?" Brownie fidgeted, all psyched up for battle with no one to fight.

"I know so," Stowe said in a grateful rush. He had just spied Karla trudging up the street with a sack of groceries in her arms.

Brownie leaped to his feet, grinning. "What did you buy at the store?" he called. "A new face, on sale?"

"Oh, Brownie, clever you," Karla said, turning in at her own walk. She looked hot. "My grandmother's at a convention and we've got to have my grandfather for dinner three nights. My mother's gone to get him. He's such a pain. He's got enough money to have caviar casserole every meal, and we wind up cooking for him." She followed their uneasy glances to the rumpled sack between them on the step. "What've you got in *your* bag? An emergency brain?"

They glanced at each other, checking for signs of second thoughts or sagging resolve. Brownie said, "You sure missed a neat picnic yesterday."

"And we missed you," Stowe said. "Especially your cookies."

"That's funny," Karla said. "I didn't miss you two free samples at all."

"So what did you and the Kawasaki King do yesterday that was so great?" Brownie asked.

"Went to a kegger out at the lake." She flung her hair. "More beer than lake. Everybody was there."

"We weren't," Stowe said.

"Now you know what separates the men from the boys." She came closer. "Move over, I've got to go in."

"Don't you ever feel dumb?" Stowe asked before he could stop himself.

"What kind of choice remark is that?"

"I mean — I mean, don't you ever feel stupid with people that age, not knowing things?"

Karla sized him up through the celery sticking out of her sack. "I'd rather feel stupid now than when I'm seventeen, if that's what you mean."

"You would?" It seemed to him that if he were old enough to be really embarrassed, he'd also be old enough to handle it better. What he really meant, he guessed, was that he wished he could put off growing up until he was older.

"Hey, let me up the steps."

"Can't," Brownie said. "We've got our orders. Nobody passes. You're behind enemy lines."

Stowe said hurriedly, "We declared war on you, Karla. We meant to tell you yesterday at the picnic, but you didn't care to show up." He opened the sack and peeped in. The arsenal he saw made him tingle. He handed Brownie a taut, water-filled balloon as carefully as if it were a real ticking bomb.

"Oh, no, you don't," Karla warned them. "I've just washed my hair." She backed off, lifting her grocery sack like a shield. Brownie's balloon arched out and burst against it. "You clumsies," she yelled, bolting out into the street.

Stowe's balloon caught her between the shoulder blades. Her blouse turned from pink to rose. At the same moment her wet sack opened like bomb-bay doors and let out a rain of tomatoes and peppers.

110

"You dog-breath! Get away!" She saw Brownie aiming the can of shaving cream at her, and let the whole sack fall so she could run. Brownie lunged after her, but overshot when she ducked, and creamed a parked car instead. "Ha!" she cried in triumph.

Stowe ran up behind her with the arsenal sack and grabbed her arm, but couldn't get the ketchup bottle out without turning loose again.

Karla swung at him and missed. "Aren't you dummies ever going to grow up?"

"No!" they shouted in unison. Brownie caught her other arm. She began a long siren scream as she dragged them along. They hung on, trying to unscrew the bottle top while their sack tore and feathers spouted from it. Heads appeared at the door of the next house.

"Laugh," Brownie ordered. "Act happy or they'll think we're killing you."

"You are, dumbskull," Karla screeched.

"Numbskull," Stowe corrected, waving gaily. "Don't worry, folks — we'll have the crazy lady in custody before she terrorizes the neighborhood." He cackled. He was doing something crazy again, just like Brownie. With reckless elation he clamped one arm around Karla's waist and felt the breath whoosh out of her. For a second he was aware that, one-handed, he could hurt her if he wanted to. Then sadness filled him, for something ending. He liked her so much, and they couldn't play that way much longer. The people watching had suddenly made it forbidden, like that strange wall in Berlin that stopped people from going where they had always gone.

Karla broke free and darted back up the walk. They

snatched her to a stop before she reached her house. "Now, hey. Stop." She launched a kick that could have made kindling out of their shins. They leaped back like Scottish dancers, then close again, wrestling and gasping. "I'm serious. Stop it."

They were deaf. Momentum carried them on, screeching wildly. They had to win. They had to have victory to remember in that thinking time coming at the end. It was out of their hands.

"Ketchup," Brownie yelled. "It's tar and feather time."

Stowe struggled to hold the bottle over her head as she jerked and writhed. Ketchup hung at the bottle's neck. He banged it. A blob splashed on Brownie's nose. Nothing had ever seemed so funny. He heard his laughter, roller-coasting up and down. He liked feeling Karla's fists whack his chest. The war had been a terrific idea.

"I mean it, damn it!" Karla exploded. She jerked free again. They chased her up the sidewalk. She grabbed the screen door just as the ketchup finally gushed out. Half of the red stream hit the door frame. Half caught Karla's swinging hair and continued on into the living room. The fierce resistance suddenly dropped from her mouth, leaving it agape.

"Hey, wait—" Stowe began, but Brownie's handful of feathers poofed into Karla's face. The next blob broke like a blizzard against the screen as she slammed it shut.

"Bullseye!" Brownie shouted.

"Wait," Stowe begged. "Hey. Stop."

He peered through the screen as Karla flung herself across the room, shedding down like a blown dandelion.

"Why?" Brownie asked, clutching the last handful of feathers.

"Because she — I don't know — she looked like she was crying."

"What for?" Brownie asked, and collided with Mrs. McWhitty coming up the steps. Behind her was a grey-haired man who looked like he might have played professional football. And still could. With them for the other team.

Mrs. McWhitty took a long whiff of ketchup and looked at the feathers. "What on earth are you doing — staging a chicken-plucking contest on my front porch?" She went past them, icy-eyed, and followed the trail of feathers down the hall.

Karla's grandfather came up the steps, getting taller and taller until Stowe and Brownie were tilting like baby birds. "What the hell were you boys trying to do to my granddaughter?" he bellowed.

They were struck speechless. It seemed so obvious, what they were doing. Brownie held out a handful of feathers, drew it back, and tried to mash it into his pocket. Stowe scooped a dribble of ketchup off the door frame and didn't know where to put it. "It's not blood," he said, hoping he wasn't giving Karla's grandfather any ideas on retribution.

"I can't believe this. I ought to call the police, right this instant," Karla's grandfather yelled. His voice was still in as good shape as the rest of him. "For assault. Assault! You cocky little terrorists — you ought to be locked up." He ran his finger up a ketchup dribble and didn't know what to do with it, either. "Look at this!"

Mrs. McWhitty came to the screen. "Dad," she said, "hush. Come inside. Karla's all right." She held the screen open until he blustered in, still balancing ketchup on his finger.

Stowe gulped. "We didn't mean to mess up your *house*." It didn't sound the way he had meant it to. "I mean—"

Mrs. McWhitty handed each of them a wet towel. "Clean up out there. I'll do the rug."

"It was just meant for fun," Brownie said in a gush. "Yesterday you were saying if we declared war—"

"I was saying nice simple shaving cream," Mrs. McWhitty said, swiping at the down on the screen.

"You'll pick up every damn feather out there," Karla's grandfather said behind her. He shoved two paper sacks out at them. "Look at that yard. An exploded henhouse. Look at this screen. Vandalism!"

"Dad," Mrs. McWhitty said sharply. "Would you get the rug shampoo. Please!"

"Is Karla okay?" Stowe asked.

"She will be," Mrs. McWhitty said. "Right now she's in the shower, crying her head off and plugging the drain with feathers."

Stowe looked at Brownie. The excitement oozed out of him, leaving a nightmarish stillness. Maybe it was a dream and hadn't happened. Brownie's pocketful of feathers had to be a dream. So did the task of picking up every wisp of down drifting across the porch and into the grass. He began to giggle in helpless dream-laughter.

Mrs. McWhitty, on her hands in a froth of rug shampoo, said, "Gather up everything you can. Then come back in the morning and finish."

Stowe brushed the molting edge of Brownie's pocket. "Brownie, you better ask if you can sleep over, so we can come back really early."

Brownie sank to his knees and scooped at a drift of feathers. The down rose and floated away. The feathers he dropped toward his sack eddied past it to the ground. "Maybe I better ask to stay two nights," he said.

Mrs. McWhitty shut the door. The porch light suddenly came on. They cringed like escapees on a prison wall. Out of the corner of his eye Stowe checked the lighted windows of his own house across the street. As he crawled through a miniature cotton field, picking puffs of down, he saw what he expected to see: Annie walking past the window toward the telephone.

The war was going to start on a new front.

They had cleaned half the porch when Karla's face suddenly appeared at her living-room window, a silhouette framed by lank wet hair. "I have something to say," she called out. They rose expectantly, grateful to have communication restored. "I hate you," she said distinctly, and yanked the curtain shut.

Stowe's breakfast was waiting, cold, the next morning, when they finished repairing the war damage and Brownie eased himself home. Stowe ate toast slowly. Annie had been in bed, or pretending to be, when he got home the night before, and he wanted to hold off a meeting as long as possible.

Finally he went to her room. She was diapering Tyler. "Out on parole?" she asked. He couldn't see her face, but her back looked angry.

"I guess so," he said carefully. "What's left in the grass looks like clover blossoms."

"I was told last night I should have better control over you. What do you suggest? Tying you to the bedpost?" She had that clipped voice that meant she was mad as a hornet. He lagged behind her to the kitchen. "Dry," she said, jerking her hand at the dishes. "Danged if I'll do your chores while you pick feathers."

He dried. Annie started the laundry, briskly working off her disappointment in him. He said, "I'm sorry you got dragged into it."

"Stowe, I have to stay neighbors with those people."

"I know. It just backfired. If that pain-in-the-butt grandfather hadn't been there—"

"Don't blame grandfathers. It's *you* who have to know when something's going too far."

Through the front window he saw the Kawasaki King rumble to a stop in front of Karla's house. A moment later, Karla bounced down the walk, being careful not to look across the street, and got on behind him. The King glanced over, making what Stowe was sure was a smirk behind his helmet.

"Have you apologized yet?" Annie asked.

The King goosed the throttle for a show-off exit. Abruptly, to Stowe's deep satisfaction, he popped the clutch and killed the engine. With Karla's extra weight on the back he couldn't get started. She squeezed out between him and the sissy bar, and stood seething as the King kicked his starter lever over and over. Stowe watched contentedly until the engine finally coughed to a start. Karla squeezed on again, and they wavered off.

"I told her mother I was sorry," he said. "Not her. Why should I?"

"It might be nice to be friends again."

"I don't want to be," he said. He gazed after them, watching Karla tilt wrong at the corner as usual, with her arms tight around the Kawasaki King. "That lazy air-brain's never even bothered to get a helmet for her. If he was any smarter he could be a brick."

Annie said, "People mature at different speeds, you know. Some just turn loose their childhood earlier than others. So don't take it out on Karla because she's moving on ahead of you into new country."

He shot her a suspicious glance. She was always picking up on his real emotion. She made him feel transparent. It had been great, going to war against Karla. Just pow-pow like the old roughhousing days. Just the easiness together that he didn't want to lose. But he could sense her trying to make something more out of it, like everybody else.

"People always seem to give this kind of thing a sexual connotation," she said.

He gulped, afraid to ask what *that* was. "It was supposed to be funny! I don't know why it all went backwards."

"Stowe, you've got to listen to people. When they say No, stop. Try to feel out, and understand what they're wanting or needing, for goodness sake."

So feel out to me, he wanted to say. Understand how it was. He asked recklessly, "How come you're always giving advice, when you got so messed up with your own life?"

She said, "I may have messed up my life, but I put ketchup on hamburgers."

He gave her back her level stare. Slowly they shifted into the balance, the oneness that filled him with peace.

She said, "Mrs. McWhitty thinks you owe Karla an apology."

"Do you?"

She almost smiled. "I tend to take your side of things. But, sure, apologize. Why not? It'll strengthen your character."

He thought about new country. Maybe it wasn't as scary or complicated as he thought. He had gone into plenty of new country with Annie, and had never been afraid. New towns, different houses, but always part of the same safe team, the two-headed turtle in a shell.

He guessed what had angered him in Karla was the way she had taken off alone without any road map, or any hesitation, or any sign of the fear he felt.

Slowly he shook his head. "No," he said. He wasn't going to apologize to anyone who kept reminding him every dog-breath day that he was expected to take off into that new country himself, before he even knew how to drive.

When Stowe got home from a combination lawn-mowing and car-wash on Wednesday, Annie was hunched over her quilting frame, finishing up the World-Without-End she was making for somebody's king-size bed. He could tell by her face that there was no Aunt Fritzi letter yet. So what could he say? There were no letters from his contests, either, saying Congratulations . . .

118

"What's cool to eat?" he asked, wiping his sweaty face.

"Nothing." Annie thumped the bulge that Yetta's head made when she stood up under the quilt. "Down, Yetta-bug. You'll get your head quilted." She jumped and pricked her finger as Tyler stood on her bare toes.

"Down, Tyler," Yetta said, helpfully knocking him to the floor. He lay startled a moment, watching his bottle roll under the couch, and began a long leisurely scream. Annie sighed and took him in her arms.

"You're all right," she assured him, signaling Stowe to fish out the bottle. "My baby boy. It's hard to be little, isn't it? I wish you had a big blowzy mother to hold you. I wish you didn't have to love a plastic bottle."

Tyler trailed off, comforted, and smoothed the warm slope of her breast with his little sausage fingers. Stowe looked away, remembering that slope.

"Sorry. It doesn't work anymore," she told Tyler. "When old Stowe was your age we had a real dairy going. For so long that when I finally said, You've got to be weaned, *he* said, Whadda you mean, weaned?"

"Mom, you're weird," Stowe said, embarrassed.

She laughed. Tyler, feeling it, opened his mouth, too, and bared his jack-o-lantern teeth. Stowe dragged himself to his room, dropping his grass-stained sneakers as he went. He fell across his bed. Immediately Yetta crawled up, too, and sat on his stomach.

"Hey," he mumbled. "I'm tired." He raked her off, and she curled up beside him.

"Stowe, you know what? There was a kitty up a tree, and Annie couldn't get it down. I think it was going to build a nest."

Stowe jerked a little laugh. The nice thing about instant little sister was that she gave him nights and weekends off, to build up patience for the days she was there.

He was almost dozing when he heard Tyler paddling in the toilet bowl. "Mom," he groaned. He heard her push her chair back. He guessed he should have tackled Tyler himself, so she could get the quilt done. She was always rushing to finish a crib blanket, or stuffed toys. For years she had promised him a Double Monkey Wrench for his bed, and never had the time to make it.

"You know what?" Yetta said. "It was a girl kitty. Its father came over and called, and when it came down he said, Good girl."

He opened his eyes. A warm wave of disbelief rose slowly over him and dropped, cutting off his breath. He sat up. His hundred-dollar bill was gone.

He slid silently off the bed and touched the wall. The tacks were gone. The play money framed an oblong space.

Numbly he patted the floor, the cluttered top of his desk. Then in a frenzy he looked everywhere. Under the bed. In drawers. It had fallen. It had blown somewhere. He cried out soundlessly, Oh, God, please — where's my money!

"Yetta," he whispered, catching her shoulders. "Remember the paper that was up there, like money? Did you take it down?"

"Where?" she asked, staring, the dumb way all little kids did, in every direction but where he meant.

"Up there!" He aimed her at the spot with a shake.

"Oh, you can't fool me," she giggled. "It's still up there, Stowe!"

Slowly he turned her loose, and clamped his hands over his churning stomach instead.

He searched the room again. Under the covers, in case a gust of wind had caught it while he was sleeping. Behind the furniture. Everywhere. Until there was nowhere else to look.

Somebody had taken it. There was no other explanation.

Yetta laboriously put on his sneakers. He sat down on the bed and watched their big empty heels flop as she walked, and was suddenly so tired he could cry.

"When I'm big like you," Yetta said, "I won't throw up so much, will I?"

He went into the front room where Annie sat stitching the quilt-top to its backing. "Did you take my hundred dollars down?"

She picked up a little row of stitches with her needle and glanced up. "Your funny money? I've already got wallpaper I like. Why?"

"Then somebody took it."

"What do you mean?" She stopped sewing. "Wait a minute — you can't just accuse people of taking things from your room. How do you even know what's missing from a room that messy?"

"Because I looked! And it's gone."

"So? What's the big deal?"

He opened his mouth, and couldn't tell her. Anger blazed up into his cheeks. "Why aren't you asking who did it, instead of all that mother stuff? Who's been in my room?"

She stared at him, sucking a finger she had pricked. "In your room? For heaven's sake, Stowe — "

"It was there when Brownie spent the night," he said. "We looked at it. We pretended what we'd do with it." He gulped hard. "If it was real, I mean."

Annie scraped back her chair, and stood up, winding her watch without looking at it. On the couch, Tyler turned the pages of a floppy magazine, whispering, Oh, ohhh, in his little safe world.

"So who else?" he repeated. "Besides Brownie." He uncurled his fist, ready to count fingers. Karla had seen it. Yetta's mother was always going in to find Yetta's shoes. Sir Landlard had a key and could come in, or send someone in to make an estimate or something while Annie was in the garden. Tyler couldn't reach it, but Yetta could. Or somebody off the street.

So who did he run up to first, and punch in the nose?

"Good grief, you can't add people up like that," Annie said to his hand. She stood uncertainly a moment, and went down the hall. He wondered if she was searching his room for herself. Or checking the trash baskets or vacuum cleaner, so she could come in waving it with a big I-told-you-so smile.

She came back, holding her purse. He tensed. "Look, I'm sorry," she said. "I didn't realize it was all that important to you. It's natural to wonder, when something disappears." She rubbed her forehead. "But, Stowe, can we postpone this? I've *got* to go get that grease trap. I've had a bucket under that leak for a month, and this morning it finally gave way completely, all over my cleaning powder. Will you watch the kids, or shall I take them with me to the hardware?"

He stared at her, unable to make the sudden leap into ordinary life that she seemed to have made. He knew the world had to go on running. It hadn't stopped when he saw an empty spot on his wall. But a little more sympathy would have helped.

Only, how sympathetic could he expect her to get over what she thought was a lost piece of paper?

He was stupid. Stupid! How could he have been so — so young? To let himself be robbed, and then not even be able to talk about it.

Annie slid into her sandals. "Before you know it, you'll be driving off on errands for me." She smiled uncertainly, trying, he supposed, to remind him that changes were coming that would compensate for silly little upsets like this one. Tiredly he sat down and squeezed himself small in the corner of the couch.

"I'll keep the kids," he said.

He watched her drive away. With Horseless gone, he could look across the street at the window where Karla's wet-haired silhouette had appeared. Karla wouldn't have taken it, even after the war. Saying she hated him didn't mean she did. She had hated him the first time they met and he padlocked her to the fire hydrant. She had said it when he cut the spoke on her bicycle to get her foot out. It didn't mean she hated him. She was his first friend.

Brownie wouldn't have, either. Brownie had taken one hard look at it and whispered, Stowe, it's real. Wow, that's neat. I'm going to save up my money till I can do

123

that, too. They had smiled, understanding each other. He just couldn't believe Brownie would risk their friendship for a measly hundred dollars. And Yetta's mother was Annie's friend. She trusted her little girl to them, and trust had to work both ways.

Anyway, how could he *ask* anybody? And even if he did accuse them, wouldn't it be like he said when they found the twenty-dollar bill? Who'd tell him the truth when he asked?

He wished he hadn't remembered that. If *he* hadn't hesitated to take money that wasn't his, why should he expect other people to be different? Everybody grabs and runs. He stared out the window, weighed down by depression. The world sucked.

So what was he going to do? Nothing, as usual? Let somebody have a hundred dollars, free-gratis? He needed Annie to talk to. But he couldn't have talked, even if she were there. He couldn't even say a simple thing like, It was real, and only Brownie knew it.

He went slowly to the phone, and stood a long time, twisting and untwisting the cord. Finally he dialed a number.

"Did you take my hundred dollars?"

He heard a ringing that was either distance or the blood in his ears. Then Brownie snorted. "*Take* it? Jeez. What do you think?"

"Somebody did."

They listened to each other's breathing.

"Well, I didn't," Brownie said. He gave a pained jolt of laughter. "I haven't even been *over* there, Stowe. I've been writing this stupid book thing for this afternoon." The defensive slope of his voice changed. "I don't need your hundred dollars."

Stowe shivered. His tongue went numb. He stared in wonder at the receiver, as if it were a gun he had just pointed at someone.

"Jeez, why would you even have to ask me?" Brownie said.

"I thought, maybe, like a joke — " He held a mouthful of words, like alphabet soup that he couldn't arrange. "Somebody took it." He hung up.

Before he could stiffly turn away, the phone rang.

"Hey, listen," Brownie said loudly, "why would I take your cheap hundred dollars? I've got a savings account. I don't need your money."

"Okay," Stowe breathed.

"So what do you want? You want to come over while I'm at this stupid club and search my room, or what? You want to come over tonight and ask my folks if I'm suddenly acting rich, or what?"

"I don't want to do anything," Stowe whispered.

"Okay, then." Brownie's breath hissed sharply for a second. "So don't bother me about it. Okay? If you have to ask, is that being friends? If we can't be friends, just don't bother me, okay?"

Stowe felt the receiver drop like a rock.

He scrawled a note to tell Annie where they were, and took the kids for a walk. They went through the alleys so Yetta could collect beer bottles and dead bugs and weeds. Tyler staggered along behind them in his crinkling diaper, stopping occasionally to taste-test a pebble. Stowe walked

125

in slow motion so they could keep up, carefully holding his mind as empty as the burning sky.

When they got back, Annie was under the sink, putting in the new grease trap. He had just stepped silently over her stuck-out feet, to go back outside, when she said from inside the cabinet, "Hi, want to help?"

He hesitated. Usually he liked repairing things. But not this time. "No," he said.

Her head came out. She blinked up at him, smearing pipe joint compound on her ear as she pushed her hair back. "I take it things haven't improved for you."

"No, they haven't. They're worse."

She brought out the old, rusted curl of pipe. "All right," she said firmly. "Let's have it. What's the matter?"

"Nothing's the matter — nothing as important as fixing the sink." He edged toward the door.

"Stowe. Get back here. You're playing a big dramatic scene and I don't understand what it's about. If you're mad at me because you think I let people poke around in your room — "

"You let them sleep there. You must let them poke, too, because my money's gone."

She got up and opened the faucet a dribble to test her new connections. "You keep yelling *money* like it was real."

"It was!" he yelled.

Her eyes grew round. "It was real?"

"It was a hundred dollars. Don't you understand? Real! I saved up all year. Then I added that twenty."

She let the water run, forgetting it. "Stowe. But I thought — " Her face experimented with different expressions. "Why on earth did you stick it up there on the *wall* if it was real?"

He knew she would ask that, and he wouldn't be able to explain. Why had he? Because it made him feel safe? Powerful? Because it was his, to decide about, all by himself? "Just to look at," he said.

"Oh, no," she said softly. He could almost imagine her mind calculating the food and gas and rent increases it could have paid for. Her eyes kept blinking in a jumbled Morse code. "But, Stowe — were you afraid I'd ask to share it, or what? Did you think you had to lie about it?"

"I didn't think I had to do anything about it — till somebody took it!"

"But why didn't you say it was real? I would have made you put it in a safe place. Obscenity! I'm so used to trusting you, I automatically believed Ben Franklin was flying his kite on a counterfeit bill."

Water began to drain from the joint of the new pipe she had put in.

"Oh, damn," she exclaimed, twisting the faucet shut. She grabbed a cuptowel and disappeared into the cabinet to wrap it around the spewing connection.

Stowe turned toward the door again.

Her head reappeared. "Wait a minute. I want to talk. But this thing — " She groped for her wrench.

"Sure," he said, and kept on walking.

He sat in the kids' little swing, feeling shaky. His feet dragged back and forth as he stared over the roofs at the mountains fading to smoke in the afternoon haze. Gradually he calmed himself and listened for Annie's footsteps, half of him hoping she would come, and half of him hoping she wouldn't.

The sun slid behind the mountains. He heard water spattering loudly in the sink and knew she had got the leak stopped and was fixing supper. There was a soft clatter at the front door as the kids were picked up. Then a silence.

Annie came out and handed him a sandwich. She sat down against the tree trunk with a sandwich of her own, and gave him a wan smile. "You okay?"

He shrugged, pressing his shoulders into the scratchy rope.

"Stowe," she said tautly, "I'm really sorry. About your money. I didn't realize, when I was riding you about throwing a scene." She peeled the crust from her bread, not really looking at him. "I know how you feel. It's hard, I know. A real calamity."

"You don't know," he said. But he guessed maybe she did, in a way. Every month all the money she had disappeared to pay the bills. He sighed. "If I just knew it was lost somewhere, and nobody took it."

"Oh, don't think somebody took it, Stowe."

"Well, what do I think? I want my money back."

"I know." She ate in silence. All of a sudden she stood up. "Listen, what kind of cake would you like?"

He stared at her strangely. They had cake four times a year. For their birthdays, and Yetta's and Tyler's. "What for?" he asked. "To celebrate Stupid Day? Whodunit Day?"

"No. To try to make I'm-Sorry-It-Happened Day a little better."

In spite of himself he said, "The kind with banana-and-pineapple stuff between the layers?"

"Perfect." She made a quick uncertain smile. "Hey, what rule says you get to sit and mope while I do all the drudging? Come cream the sugar. Okay?"

He followed her numbly into the kitchen and sat on the stool he had used before he could reach the table from a chair. They had always shared the kitchen, baking clay and bread in the same oven, cooking around tools and paint and sawdust. Once she decorated Christmas cookies with his salmon eggs by mistake.

"I called Aunt Fritzi a few minutes ago," Annie said, bringing out the bowls.

He felt himself drop, like the people at carnivals who got ducked in a tank of water. For a moment he couldn't breathe. It had happened. The way he had dreaded it would. All those days, and then she hadn't even waited for low rates.

He surfaced with a silent gasp. "Did she say anything about—" He stopped and steadied his voice. "About how he's feeling?"

"She said he wasn't doing well. He's very weak. Stowe. I've got to go visit him."

He knew what it felt like to be chased into a dead-end alley. He could feel cold stone all around him. "You really like going out of your way to get yourself hurt again, don't you?"

"Hey, stow it, Stowe," she said. "It took all the courage I had to reach out and touch those people again."

She looked so sad and tired he was sorry he had said it.

Mechanically he mashed the sugar and margarine she had given him.

"I realized something down there under the sink," she said, sifting flour. He mashed, trying to imagine what. "I realized that the chance to reconcile with my dad was going to be gone someday, and all those fine feelings of forgiveness and understanding wouldn't have done him any good hanging there on my wall. I realized I'd look up someday and he'd be gone, just like your hundred dollars."

He felt a tingle of guilt. "I would have let you take the money if you needed it. I meant to."

"I expect you would have, Stowe. Because we've always shared what we had. But I saw something. We're both becoming hoarders. We've lived so tight and done without so long, we've started hoarding everything we have. That's no way to live. Money has to be translated into life-giving things. Like food and books and home. Or it's worthless."

"I would have spent it," he said, miserable.

"Well, you didn't. Stowe, we're hoarding *ourselves*, too. I can see it, because I've been scared so long, afraid to risk myself or spend myself."

"So you called," he said, watching her mix milk and flour. His thoughts must look clotted like that. Thankfulness that Aunt Fritzi hadn't known about Harold's call. Fear that he was caught at the end of the alley anyway. "Just like that."

"I told her we'd come."

He went rigid. "Well, we can't. What about Yetta and Tyler?"

"I've already found somebody who'll take them while we're gone."

"But we still can't," he said.

She dusted flour across the greased cake pans and let what didn't stick fall off into the sink. "Why not?"

"Because," he said desperately. "We don't need him. Or his charity money either. Why can't we just forget about him, like he did us?"

She poured the batter. "Stowe. Do you realize this may be the last chance you'll have to see your grandfather?"

"That can't make me like him," he said.

"Can't it *stretch* you a little bit, for heaven's sake?" She handed him the batter bowl. "Could Brownie take your route while we're gone?"

He held the bowl, that was usually so good to lick, feeling doomed.

"Oh, Stowe. What? You accused Brownie of taking your money."

He nodded, almost welcoming the detour she had suddenly taken. "We're not friends anymore."

"Oh, Stowe. You didn't." Her eyes went round and dark. "You couldn't have. Not Brownie. Oh, you poor idiot boy."

Before he could stop himself, he hit her hand that had been reaching out to touch him. "Just get away and let me alone," he yelled. "I hate this. I hate being all mixed up like this!"

She held her slapped hand under her chin like a little animal he had hurt. "Damn it, I have to tell you something."

"No you don't! I've lost my money and you trusted me

131

about it, and Brownie and Karla don't like me, and now you want me to go to Oklahoma and forgive some man for the way he messed up your life. You're weird!" He couldn't take his eyes off her red hand beneath her drained-white face. He nibbled his knuckle in regret. "I didn't mean to hit you."

She put the layers in the oven and slowly mashed bananas and pineapple in a pan. She said, "When you were little, I slapped you, sometimes. Because you were handy when I couldn't strike out at your father, or my father, or my life, or whatever was hurting me. I know you're hurting. I don't want to make it worse, but I've got to. I know where the money went. Yetta was cutting it into little pieces one day, and when I started to scold her she threw up on it, and I gathered everything up and flushed it down the john."

For a long time he only stared. Inside his head, questions like race cars shuddered in a row, waiting to roar off. Suddenly he let the first one go.

"Why'd you lie?"

"Oh, Stowe, I didn't outright lie. I was — I just protected myself."

"But you didn't tell me what had happened. When I asked you!"

"I know! I didn't. But I hadn't thought it was serious until you said the money was real. And suddenly I felt so scared and stupid and — and *duped* — "

"You could have saved the *pieces*," he yelled. "The bank would take pieces and give you back a whole one!"

"I know that — but try to get it through your head I thought it was fake."

"Jeez," he exclaimed. "Make it all my fault."

"It wasn't all your fault. It was Yetta's fault and my fault. *And* your fault. That's why I had to have time to think — before we were suddenly yelling at each other, all flared up over who's to blame —"

She grabbed up the damp dishcloth and cooled her face with it, leaving a little banana-string caught in the edge of her hair. At the sight of it his anger slowly melted into a small leaden drop of sadness. It was all gone. His power. Flushed away. The oneness he loved to feel with her. Brownie's friendship. All gone.

"I'm sorry," Annie said. "I feel awful. I was to blame. When I realized you had accused Brownie, I just — I'm very sorry. I should have admitted what had happened, and not waited."

He felt his scalp prickle at the echoes in her last words. He got up, distressed, and peeped at the cake layers. Sometimes they came out golden black instead of golden brown unless he helped watch.

"I couldn't let you go leaping onto Yetta. She was perfectly innocent — you have to understand that," she said. "She was listening the day Karla joked about taking five dollars' worth. She was cutting it up to give to all of us. You and me and Tyler. And some for her mother. She cried when I said it was too yucky to save." Suddenly she was making a strangled kind of laugh. "Oh, Stowe, this is too ridiculous. How do these things happen to us?"

"I don't know," he said.

"I'm sorry. Really and truly. What else can I say?"

"Nothing," he said. He crunched himself small on the stool. "I'm sorry, too. But, jeez. My money."

"I know." She smiled so sadly that he was sure she did.

"It was my fault first," he said.

"No. Forget fault. Nobody did anything on purpose to hurt anyone else. It was just one of those crazy bad-sad things that happen. One of the misters."

"The what?"

"Misters. When you were little. Remember? That's how you pronounced mysteries. For the longest time I couldn't figure what you mean when you'd tell me something was a big mister."

Something occurred to him. She hadn't had to admit what she'd done — that she'd tried to let it slide and not get blamed. She could have left it a big mister and never risked a thing. He wondered if she knew that was pretty brave.

He looked at the cake again. "It looks ready," he said. "Don't you think it's ready?"

She got out her little wire racks. "Stowe, can you call Brownie and apologize? I will, too. Then will you ask him if he'll do your papers while we're gone?"

Without warning she had dropped him into the water tank again. "I don't want to go to Oklahoma." He grabbed a breath. "You're not going to change somebody that's blocked you off all these years — it's a waste of time and money."

"Oh, Stowe, let's don't start that," she said.

"You're not listening to me!" He could feel words vibrating far away in him, like a train that had been coming for days, and had finally arrived. "I'm not going. We can't go."

"I can."

"No. Listen. You can't. Aunt Fritzi's Harold called me on the phone. About your dad. Your dad doesn't want you. He wants me."

She stood with the cake layers in her hands, blinking as if he had flung his fist at her again.

"What?" she said. "I don't understand."

"Your cousin Harold said your dad was asking for me. He wants me to come." The astonishment widening her eyes melted his strength. "I didn't want to tell you," he said, and took the cake pans out of her hands.

She sat down. "He asked for you?"

He nodded. "But if he can't ask for both of us —"

"Not me?" Her voice was small behind the hand she had put to her mouth. "Nothing about me?"

"Listen, he can't just give me a summons, like a policeman. Doesn't he know we're a team? If he can't ask for both of us —"

"Not me," she said. She put her hands out on the hot pans and didn't know it.

"Listen, just forget it," he coaxed, wondering how they'd ever be able to trust each other after this crazy night. "I was right not wanting to tell you. I knew you'd just be sadder."

"He doesn't even know you," she said in a flat zombie voice. "He wouldn't recognize you on the street, his only grandson."

He waited, unable to gather what she was getting at.

"That's cruel," she said. "That's cruel. To pick you. Who does he think he is — God? He can't just pick people

135

like daisy petals — love you, love you not! I'm his daughter. I'm his Annie. What did I do so terrible that I have to pay for it thirteen years?"

"Nothing." The pain in her eyes when she turned to him scared him more than her words. "You haven't done anything. Don't let him do that to you. Please. He's not worth it. You don't have to let him."

"Why would he use you to hurt me?" she asked. "What's he trying to do?"

"What does it matter? He's just a mixed-up old bitter man."

She stared at him as if she were trying to remember who he was. Her voice dropped. "Oh, Stowe. He is."

"And he doesn't own us — "

"He is," she said. Her voice went soft. "He's getting old. He's a lonely old man, and he doesn't know I love him."

"But you don't," he said. "You don't. I knew this would happen if I told you."

"He's not strong anymore," she murmured, not hearing him. "And it's scary. And he's reaching out to you. Oh, Stowe. He's reaching out to you."

He sprang up. The kitchen was too hot. There was nothing to breath but stifling feelings. He said, "I don't want him reaching for me. That makes me feel guilty. Jeez! I didn't ask for that. It's awful, when it's something you want so bad and I don't."

"I wasn't thinking. It was such a slap in the face, I wasn't thinking." To his amazement she smiled. "This is a wonderful thing. He wants you."

"But not *you!*" he yelled.

"I know, I understand that. But it's such a beginning! Don't you know the happiness it would give me for you and your grandfather to come together?"

He stared at her, baffled. She had flipped the whole meaning like a pancake, mixing him all up.

She stood up. "Oh, I wish you could have told me, child. We could have started planning the minute Harold called." She pulled a pencil and a scrap of paper from a drawer. "I'll call again. I know we can't leave tomorrow. But the next morning — early. And be there that night." He watched her scribble. *Cancel nursery. Brownie sub. Arrange T and Y.*

"Now wait a minute," he exclaimed. "Don't I have any say? You can't just shove me back and forth like playing checkers. You or him either. I'm not going."

She gazed at him. "You can't mean that."

"I can mean it. I don't want to know him. This is your mess, not mine. It's been ten or twelve days. You didn't even have the nerve to call. Now all at once we can't wait another minute, because you've got me for a wedge to stick in the door."

"Oh, Stowe, it's not that at all. How can I make you understand?" She held out the scrap of paper with an urgency that made him brace himself. "If I can risk going when I haven't been asked, can't you even go when you're wanted?"

"No," he said.

"Why? Why? It's such a chance! If I had it — " She swept past him down the hall.

He heard the bathroom door slam. She cried there, sometimes, when things were bad. This was bad. He sat

137

down, wishing it were over, and slowly nibbled little mousy crumbs of cake.

Annie bent over the quilt all day, stitch, stitch, stitch, wiping dots of blood from her punctured fingers. Stowe took over Yetta and Tyler, and did the laundry and watered the garden, keeping out of Annie's way, silent and withdrawn, while anxiety clamored inside him louder than the kids. She searched his face, but he was not ready to show her anything, and turned away.

He mowed two lawns after he had delivered his papers, striding, heavy with apprehension, through the endless grass. He wondered what she was thinking as she sewed. Did those little startled pricks mean she was recalling her surprise, or anger, or her disappointment in him?

It had been a strange new experience, suddenly saying what he would or wouldn't do. It was almost like having his money back. He guessed wanting that power was what had made him dig in his heels and say No. Even when Yes would have been the right word.

An awful thought occurred to him. What if he had said yes, and they went, and he met the man who had caused all this, and liked him?

When he pushed his mower home from the cat lady's house he saw that he had forgotten his can of gasoline. He went back for it, and somehow kept on walking slowly through the slender afternoon shadows in the direction Brownie lived. From the corner he could see Brownie batting a tennis ball against the garage door. He stopped, feeling queasy. Brownie missed a swing with his baseball bat, spun around, and saw him.

Stowe lifted the gas can in a little gesture of greeting. Brownie came to the curb. He balanced the bat upright on his finger a second, and let it pitch forward into the yard.

Stowe came closer, lifting the gas can again. "Finished the cat lady."

"Yeah?" Brownie said.

With a rush of hope Stowe said, "Did you get your book report done?"

"Yeah," Brownie said.

"I thought about calling you, but I figured you were at that club thing."

"That was yesterday," Brownie said. He sat on the curb and picked his scabs from the day they built the dam. Stowe sat the right distance away and waited. Brownie pointed to the gas can. "Let me see that."

Stowe passed it to him. Brownie unscrewed the cap and poured gasoline over the tennis ball. "Hey," Stowe said. "Don't do that."

"Why?"

"Because that gas is for business, not playing around with."

"So take it off your income tax." Brownie stood up and opened a book of matches.

"Hey," Stowe said, scrambling up too. "Hey, don't."

Brownie pitched a lighted match at the ball. They both jumped back as flame burst around it in a gush of sound.

"Dummy — stomp it out," Stowe said, too fascinated to move. The ball burned like things in a war, shimmering eerily in its island of fire.

Brownie went toward it, and suddenly began to laugh, pointing down. They were both barefooted. He grabbed

139

the bat and smashed it down on the ball. The ball shot sideways and hit the curb, leaving a spot of fire. They both doubled up with laughter, and pranced around, dodging the bat as Brownie pounded the skittering ball. Suddenly he took a giant golf swing and sent it flying down the street.

"Oh jeez," he gasped.

A dark car, just passing at the end of the block, slowly backed up and turned into his street.

"Patrol car," Stowe breathed. Instantly he was galloping across the lawn behind Brownie, still clutching his gas can. They crashed through the back door and slammed it behind them. From a bedroom window they could see a policeman in a blue uniform coming up the walk. A big black leather holster bulged at his side. They heard him knock.

"Are you going?" Stowe whispered.

"But we didn't do anything," Brownie whispered back. "No cars were coming or anything. It would have stopped burning in another minute."

The second knock was louder. "You're supposed to go to the door," Stowe said, not sure where he had got that specific information.

"Well, I'm not going to the door," Brownie whispered. "He'd just want to see my folks, anyway. Let him come back when they're home."

They watched until the officer got into his car and drove away. Stowe took a long breath. "Do you think we're in trouble? I think maybe he just wanted to scare us. For our own good." He gave Brownie a glance. "Because it wasn't a really smart thing to do. We could've got hurt, messing with gasoline."

Brownie shrugged, almost anxious enough to agree. "But fun," he said, with his wagging-puppy smile.

In spite of himself, Stowe smiled back. "Yeah. Boom! Just like a flame thrower."

They went into the silent living room and stared out more boldly to be sure the car was out of sight. The street had a little black spot on it.

"Your folks don't work this late, do they?" Stowe asked.

"They're at a meeting about trying to get a pay raise." Brownie led the way back to the kitchen and opened the refrigerator. "Want a beer?" He pulled the tab on a can.

Stowe hesitated. It looked good, but root beer was as far as Annie went. They had brewed their own home-made kind the summer before, and the bottles blew their corks in the middle of the night. He almost put out his hand, tempted, and drew it back, making a laugh. "I better not. I've got to walk home."

Brownie drank from the can. As if he had just thought about it, he said, "So your hundred bucks turned up missing."

Stowe lifted his shoulders. He had almost forgotten what he had come for. "Yeah. It did."

"Jeez, I'd be finding out who did it," Brownie said.

"You would?" he asked. "How?" He was truly curious. How would you know if it had been a weird little kid who threw up when she was scared, or a weird mom who flushed money down the toilet, or the weirdest dumbo of all who stuck his money on the wall?

141

Brownie scowled at him. "I'd just find out, that's all!"

Stowe almost smiled, because Brownie with all his bluster wouldn't have known the answer either. He felt calmness close over him, like the times in winter when the wind dropped and the silent snow began to fall. "Yetta cut it up in little pieces, and it got thrown out."

"Jeez," Brownie said, incredulous. "I'd kill the kid."

"She didn't know any better," Stowe said. "She's little."

"Little! So's a poison dart. But your money's gone, just the same, isn't it? Aren't you even mad about it?"

"Sure I'm mad. I could eat rocks. And I feel stupid. And — and — " He didn't suppose there was a word for feeling picked out by fate for a crash course in growing up. "And sad," he said. "But what am I supposed to do, now that it's over? Except maybe try to learn a hundred dollars' worth from what went wrong."

"I'd still kill her," Brownie said, flattening his empty can. "You're strange, Stowe. Really strange." He handed him a leftover pork chop.

Stowe took a big bite and swallowed hard. "Anyway, it wasn't you, and I'm sorry and I apologize. That's what I came over for. Because being friends back again is — " He felt his stupid eyes sting. "I was really dumb. I know you wouldn't take my money."

"Hey," Brownie said, embarrassed. "Not all that dumb. I thought about it."

They stared, relieved, into each other's eyes. And even while their small shy grins of trust grew larger, it occurred to Stowe that he didn't know if Brownie had said that to share his burden with him, or because it was true. There was always one mister left.

They went to the kitchen door and made sure the back of the house hadn't been staked out. Now that they could talk freely to each other again, they wandered down the alley in silence, peacefully gnawing pork chops.

At the end of two blocks, Brownie said, "You see Karla yet?"

"When she took off with the Kawasaki King yesterday. She wouldn't look at me." They went on, leaving their bones for a cat peering out of a garage. "You know what we ought to do? Take her some flowers."

"Oh, pathetic," Brownie said, wiping his hands on somebody's fence.

"This kind of flowers." Stowe snapped the stem of a dry weed. Seeds and dead leaves dropped with a rustle. Slowly Brownie matched his smile, imagining the possibilities. He lifted a wilted rhubarb leaf from a compost heap. "That's what I mean," Stowe said. "A really nice bouquet."

They began to gather all the weeds and prunings and mummified tops of discarded houseplants they could find. Gingerly they added an uprooted thistle, and tied the scraggly clump together with a cast-away sock. "Beautiful," Brownie murmured. "She's going to love it."

They held it between them as they knocked on Karla's door.

Mrs. McWhitty came to the screen. In the twilight dimness she was just a blur of grey. Then they heard her giggle. "Well, I see you've worked up to an apology."

They bobbed their heads, grinning. She called out, "Karla, you have company."

They heard the clop of wooden-soled sandals. She's expecting the Kawasaki King, Stowe thought happily. The clippity-clop stopped.

"Oh, no," Karla said, through her mother's giggles. "I thought you meant real human beings."

"They've brought you a peace offering," Mrs. McWhitty said.

Karla's face came close to the screen. "That? I'll bet it's got a snake in it."

"Darn!" Brownie said. "We forgot the snake."

Mrs. McWhitty went away. They beamed into Karla's face. Her mother came back and put three ice-cream bars into Karla's hands. "Why don't you eat these out on the steps?" she asked. "The carpet, as you may remember, has just been shampooed."

"You better tell them I'm too busy," Karla said. "I was planning to count clothes hangers tonight."

Stowe said in a spurt, "We really came over to say we're sorry about the war."

"Come on," Mrs. McWhitty urged. "Out on the steps." She gave Karla a little boost through the door.

Karla handed out ice-cream bars from as far away as possible. "You guys stay six feet away from me," she said. "I don't trust you for a micro-second." She sat primly on the top step.

Brownie laid the bouquet on her knees. She removed it with curled fingers, as if she had wet polish on, making a face that would have withered it if she hadn't been too late.

144

"We knew you'd like it," Brownie said modestly.

Karla sighed. "What a set of crazies." They all looked out at the street, not sure what the next step was. The black mountains stood as sharp as tin against the last flaring blue of the sky.

"How long you plan to stay mad at us?" Stowe said.

She twirled the stick of her ice cream. "As long as it takes."

"Takes for what?" Brownie asked, sprawling on the lawn.

"For you guys to stop acting like clowns."

"Clowns?" Brownie put a weed from the bouquet behind his ear. "What does she mean?" He clamped his teeth over the stem of a dead rose. For a second Karla's mouth twitched, then went firm again.

Stowe sat in the grass and watched the sky fade. Gone, he thought. A day has died. He felt the color of his mood go softly grey. He had to go home. He had things to face.

"You've pulled a few funnies yourself," Brownie reminded Karla. "Remember the time we found the big bag of dry ice somebody had thrown away at the park and we poured water over it and it began to smoke and bubble and you told those little kids you were a mad scientist about to blow up the world?"

"I did not," she said, and smiled.

She looked really pretty, Stowe thought. She looked posed, like a commercial, with her hands locked around her knees and her hair falling just right. Not the same girl Brownie was talking about. She had changed color, too, like the sky. Deeper.

"And of course you're the world's greatest go-cart driver," Brownie said.

Karla giggled. "There you sat, on your little platter."

Suddenly they were laughing. "And Stowe sliding you out from under the van like a pizza on a paddle."

"Are you there, Stowe?" she asked him, nudging him with her foot.

"I'm here."

"Say something."

"Rubber baby-buggy bumpers."

"Rubby bubber —" Brownie flopped in the grass, laughing.

I love you, Stowe said in his heart to them. I love us for being back together again. Do you know what you've done?

"I've got to go home," he said. "My grandfather's sick. My mom wants to go see him."

"When?" Karla asked.

"In the morning." He smoothed the grass on either side of him. Beneath its softness he could feel the solid earth. "We haven't packed our clothes yet."

"Oh, come on, Stowe. Your mother can go by herself," Brownie said. "Can't she?"

"No," Stowe said. He struggled in the silence. "Because I want to go too. He asked for me. And I just thought, like tonight when I wanted to be friends with you two again, what if you hadn't let me? What if you hadn't offered, even when you could tell how much I wanted it?" He held tight to grass clumps, not sure he was making sense. "So I dread it, but it's what I want to do."

They sat without speaking again. In the house Mrs.

146

McWhitty turned on the television to get the news. They listened to the murmur of a voice. Suddenly Brownie said, "You know what we ought to do?" They looked at him, waiting to be told. "We ought to hold the war again in fifty years. Wherever we are, we ought to have a reunion back here and clobber Karla all over again."

"You'll be a slobby old guy with a beer belly in fifty years," Karla said. "You'll be so near-sighted you can't find your feathers. I'll clobber *you*."

Brownie cackled. "How about it, Stowe?"

"Why not?" Stowe said. Inside, the phone rang. He looked across the street at the lighted window to see if it was Annie. But she was sliding the finished quilt into a plastic bag. Suddenly he understood why she had worked so steadily on it all day. She could deliver it tonight, saying it was an emergency, and tomorrow they would have gasoline money. If they needed gasoline money. She would be ready when he was.

"I mean it," Brownie said. "Wherever we are in the whole world. Karla'll forget all about it, and one day this mysterious announcement will come. The Ketchup and Feather Company invites you to the Fiftieth Anniversary of the Karla War."

Mrs. McWhitty came to the screen. "Karla. Phone."

Karla didn't look around. "I heard it," she said. "Okay." Her mother went back to the news.

She said, "So they won't make feathers anymore in fifty years, and we'll have to use plastic fuzz."

Stowe and Brownie looked at each other. She rocked on the top step. Brownie said, "I don't think your grandfather will be threatening to arrest us, but your little old

147

mom will be scooting around in her jet-propelled wheel-chair."

"Putting her tea strainer over the drain in the bathtub," Karla said.

They sat in silence.

Stowe said, "Aren't you going to talk to the Kawasaki King?"

Karla rocked gently, staring out. Stowe tried to see into her eyes, but she had turned into a silhouette again against the living-room light.

"Hey," Brownie said. "We got to go anyway."

"I know," she said. She crouched on the step in a little bundle. It's all right, Stowe ached to tell her. Everything flows on. The creek. The seasons. Us. Nothing you do can stop it. You just ride the rocks. Slowly she gathered in her breath and stood up. "Okay, Ketchup and Feather Company, don't forget to send me my invitation. Okay?"

They watched as she paused at the door to fling her hair back, and went in.

"I need to go in, too," Stowe said.

"Yeah," Brownie agreed. "You've got packing. And I've probably got a cop waiting and a paper route tomorrow. Right?" They looked at the evening star.

The news report stopped. In its place Stowe could hear a siren, far away, wailing off into silence. He thought of the loud healthy man who had made them pick up feathers, who wouldn't be at the next war. And the other grandfather he would look down on, tomorrow night, who had asked for him. He was suddenly glad they were going. He took a gulp of air that lifted him like helium. "I'll see you when we get back."

"Oh, pathetic," Brownie laughed.

"What is?"

"I just thought of something." Brownie pulled himself to his feet. "In fifty years, *we're* going to be the grandfathers."

# ❧ Six ❧

For the first miles they rode in a long tense silence. Stowe watched the mountains sink away. At the beginning they had stood high in the sun, dribbled with snow icing. He could almost guess which shadowy canyons led to Sutherland's Camp.

Finally, when he turned to look through the rear window, the horizon was flat. He faced forward, squinting into the sun glaring from Horseless's faded hood.

Annie said, "When I was little, and we started home at the end of summer, I'd talk to the mountains. I'd say, Wait for me. Be there. I'll be back. And they always waited."

The highway and the land on either side stretched out, dipping for dry water courses lined with the round-headed trees of the plains. Big cattle trucks passed with a swish that rocked Horseless as it chugged steadily through the heat.

He would glance sometimes at Annie's anxious face, and then stare ahead, not knowing what to do to help, except be there.

"I guess I should try to tell you what to expect," she said at last. "Only I don't know myself. He's back in intensive care. Someone sick is — I don't know how to prepare you. He may not be alert, mentally. With tubes and things in his arms. I wish — " She got her voice steady again. "I wish you could have known him when he was natural. All big and vigorous."

He thought, Why? What was so great about that time? That's when he slammed the door on us.

"I've seen sick people on TV," he said. "It's okay."

"Oh, grr-r," Annie said suddenly. "I've got cold shivers trying to think what to tell you. Don't mention I'm there. Not at first. Just — take his hand, or something. To show him."

"Show him what?"

"To show him whatever you can feel for him, Stowe. Or try to show what I feel, if that's all you can manage."

He looked away, strained. Sure, he told her. You can tell me what to do — just rush up and say, Oh thanks for letting me be worth knowing after all these years, like you thanked Mr. Culture for loving you. But you never got up the nerve to tell him that yourself. So how come enduring was good enough for you, but I'm supposed to move and shake?

They stopped at midmorning and got self-service gas in a little sun-bleached town. Stowe watched the numbers click, seeing the little snips of his money disappearing forever.

"I'm sorry I'm so apprehensive," Annie said. "I want you to like him. I want him to like you."

He felt like a bridge she was building, so she could go back over to the way it had been. He hadn't really thought that adults wanted to do that, too.

"Aunt Fritzi is nice. My dad is her only brother and she's spoiled him and agreed with him on everything. So naturally she sees his side. But she's done her best to keep up with us and be the go-between. Keep all that in mind."

"Sure," he said.

"She'll like you. So will Uncle Otis, but he won't show it. He'll take you to the shop and let you help weld. And of course Harold is just a sweet good-ole-boy type. You'll like him. There won't be any children your age."

"It's okay," he said, wishing he could stick out his foot and trip her so she could stop. Her apprehension was catching. He dreaded the hospital part. And all those strangers who were tied into his life. He dreaded facing the emotions he had pushed back so long. His feet pressed the floor of the pickup, applying invisible brakes to slow them down, to give him time to prepare. He gazed out at the emptiness, knowing he had to deal somehow, now, this very day, with all that world out there. The road that would stop first at his grandfather would lead someday to his own father. And eventually he'd have to arrive at the hard-to-imagine point of his life where he was the father himself.

Annie said, "You don't know how much it means to me that you came, Stowe. I know it's not easy. Thank you."

"Stay left," he said. He didn't like her being so serious and grateful about something he hadn't finished yet.

"Are you sure?" She slowed uncertainly. "Numbers.

Letters. Can't they just say: Turn here for Maydell, Oklahoma?"

"Don't curve," Stowe ordered, tangled up in the map. "Don't try to figure it — just stay left. That's it." He leaned back as Horseless headed in the right direction.

"Stowe," Annie said carefully, "do you think about your father much? You don't talk about him, so I wonder."

"What's to think?" he asked.

"I don't know. I had my father those first years. We were so close." She drew a breath. "So I don't know."

"What am I supposed to think?"

"I can't tell you what you're supposed to think! Maybe you think something nobody would ever expect to think. I never expected to think I'd be grateful to him."

"For what?" he asked in surprise.

She looked surprised herself. "For rescuing me from the depths of Maydell, first, I guess. I guess I even thank him for all those years of being angry, because I knew my other feelings weren't dead, either, if I could feel anger. And finally the anger got to be like an old stump that was dying, too, with new growing things around it, covering it up." She gave him a bent smile. "But mostly I thank him for giving me you, and letting me raise you without making you the prize in a tug of war."

His surprise took a darker shape, and he almost said, So you got to do your thing and I got to do without a father. But he didn't. It had been better that way. He was sure it had. Even if there was no way now to ever know.

"That's not much to be thankful for," he said. "Being stuck with me."

153

"Well, when we discovered we couldn't agree on any of the important things like how to raise you or spend our money or who was supposed to do all the compromising, your father said, We're not going to work out together — I want to try it alone. And off he went. So you and I inherited each other, ready or not, and I've shaped your life and you've shaped mine because of it. But you were never, never a burden, Stowe. You were my joy. You were more than enough. You made up for everything."

They slowed and crawled through a narrow town at the posted speed limit, passing a row of old men on a bench in the shade of the only tree.

Annie made a little catch of sound like a laugh. "I thought it was marriage I wanted and needed and would be good at. I didn't ever imagine I'd turn out to be a mother-freak. But how could I help it, with such a great kid?"

"You couldn't," Stowe agreed with mock solemnity.

She said shyly, "I've enjoyed you so much, Stowe. Watching you grow and change. I've had a second chance at all the things I missed in my own childhood. You've been so good, and tried so hard to please me. And done without so many things."

He wiggled, feeling glad and embarrassed at the same time. "Not too many things. It always felt rich."

"Well, I guess it was rich. Somehow money never seemed as important as living our days the way we liked. I've been so lucky. I'll never have to say I wish I'd lived them differently with you."

They were quiet together. So many words had poured

out of her, and all he could think of was that she expected him to say things to a strange man — things that could maybe change her life around — and he didn't know the first word.

Toward noon they climbed a gentle slope that revealed endless miles of space. Far off on the edge of the world, a tiny windmill pumped water for a herd of pinhead-sized cattle.

"I was hoping for a river somewhere," Annie said. "So we could eat lunch under a tree."

Stowe unfolded the map again. "Nothing," he said.

"So how about just a plain old turn-off?" She slowed down and swerved onto a dirt road. It rose slightly to cross a railroad track, and dropped down between two stubbled wheatfields. Annie drove to a wide spot farther along and pulled off the road in case someone needed to pass.

"Think of those long, slow wagon trains creeping across all this country," Annie said. "Brave."

They got out with their sandwiches and thermos of milk, and walked up and down as they ate, swinging their cramped legs and arms. Grasshoppers leaped in the roadside weeds as they passed, making rattlesnake sounds.

Stowe gazed off into the shimmering heat. Something seemed to move in it, grey and slow. "Hey," he said. "The train's coming."

They watched it take shape as it neared, a swaying freight made up of boxcars and empty coal gondolas. Stowe moved a few steps toward it, munching corn chips and cake in alternate bites, thinking of Karla chugging across the scariness of her new country. He raised his hand and waved.

Suddenly the whistle blew for the crossing, tingling his scalp with delight. "Did he see you?" Annie called. She caught up with him and they both flung their arms at the engineer, but the train carried him on, his distant face turned straight ahead.

Stowe said, "We can try again with the caboose."

They counted cars. The couplings groaned faintly as the train clicked past. They could see the little doll-house cupola swaying along like the tuft at the end of a lion's tail.

"I see somebody up there," Stowe said. They waved gleefully at the staring head in the window as the caboose lumbered by.

"We must have looked like two Mexican jumping beans in the road," Annie laughed. They started back to put the rest of the picnic behind the seat for supper.

"Why's it slowing down?" Stowe asked. They studied the train. It was creaking to a stop.

"We're still pretty close to that little town. Maybe it's some kind of local that has to wait on a siding until something important passes."

They watched it, wondering. Suddenly Stowe went rigid. He couldn't believe it. Someone was coming toward them. "Mom," he whispered, pointing. A man had left the track and was walking up the road.

"Oh, good grief," Annie said. "We've stopped a train."

They stared at each other, incredulous.

"You can't stop a *train*," Stowe informed her.

"Well, we just *did*." Annie grabbed her hair. "They

156

thought we were signaling. Hurt or something. Oh, this isn't happening. I could sink right into the ground." She caught his shoulders. "Run, Stowe. Tell him we're all right!" She gave him a shove.

He shot forward, and jolted down the road toward the man. He could see a tanned face and blue shirt. "We're sorry," he yelled. "We don't need you — we were just waving." The man stopped. Stowe began to burn with mortification. "I'm sorry."

"You're all right?" the man called.

"Oh, we're all right. Sure. Thank you." He looked back. Annie was coming, nodding and calling out the same words.

The man turned around and walked back to the train. As they watched in stunned silence it imperceptibly gathered power and moved away.

They stood in the road, red-faced. "Oh, eek," Annie said. "I'll bet we made his day."

Stowe discovered he was gripping a handful of something that had been his cake. Slowly he gathered crumbs and filling on his tongue. He couldn't look at Annie. He hadn't been so embarrassed since he tripped over the Virgin in his first Christmas pageant.

"Imagine," Annie said. A stillness had come into her face. "It stopped. A whole train stopped, just to help us. How perfectly ridiculous and wonderful."

He couldn't see the wonder part. "They must feel as stupid as we do."

"Yes, but aside from the stupidity, think of it, child. What if we *had* needed them? Do we live in a selfish, rushing, indifferent world if something like this still happens? Coo, we've got to write the railroad what a nice thing their train did."

"And get everybody fired for dumbness? It might help more if we just stopped waving like we were ship-wrecked." Stowe wiped the mixed sweat and dust off his flushed face. He longed to be safe inside Horseless. He felt exposed, watched by something laughing.

Suddenly Annie broke into a jaunty vaudeville shuffle. She touched the brim of an invisible straw hat. "All right. From now on, only the briefest hello-in-passing. Big smile. But no frantic signals to be rescued. Okay?"

Stowe felt a giggle rise like bubbles to his throat. He shuffled a quick soft-shoe step of his own in the sand of the road. With his hand almost against his chest he ventured a shy Laurel and Hardy waggle of fingers.

"Right!" Annie laughed. "Nobody would call *that* a cry for help." She grew serious. "Just think, child. This lovely kind of thing is happening all over the world every minute. Hey. No matter what it's like when we get to Maydell, Oklahoma, remember this. Okay?"

In the darkness Annie pointed out a glow in the east that was not moonrise. "There it is," she said.

Stowe jerked awake, wondering how she could know. But then, she had grown up there. She had seen that glow for more than half her life. He sat up and watched it dip away and reappear, always closer, until it became a town.

His heart began to thud with apprehension.

They drove between closed buildings striped with neon signs. He was sure it was too late to go directly to the hospital. They passed slowly under dim streetlights and stopped before a big house hidden in tree shadows. Under a long old-fashioned porch, a light burned behind a curtained window.

Annie pointed to the dark mass of another house on the other side of a wide vacant lot. "That's my dad's house, over there. That was home, where I grew up."

"Why can't we stay over there?" Stowe asked hopefully.

She hesitated. "It wouldn't seem right. Unless he invites us. You, I mean. When you see him in the morning."

"But it's your house, too."

"Not really. I left it. I chose other things."

He tried to think how it must have been, choosing the other things, someone to share life with, a home of her own. And ending up with nothing but him.

Annie patted the steering wheel gently. "You did good, Horseless." They got out and went up on the porch. A light came on above them so suddenly they almost cringed, and a little dumpy woman with dyed-red hair opened the screen and said, "Oh, Annis."

Stowe almost looked around for a third person. No one he knew called his mother by her real name. He almost expected her face to change to fit that other person, that Annis Albright, whom he had never known.

Annie took Aunt Fritzi into her arms. "This is my Stowe," she said, as they backed uncertainly apart.

"Oh, you fine-looking boy," his great-aunt said, and began to cry.

A tall stooped man appeared behind her — his great-uncle Otis, Stowe was sure — and laid his hand on

Annie's shoulder. He said, "We tried to call you this morning, but you had already left home."

"Call?" Annie said.

Aunt Fritzi said, "We knew you were on your way, so all we could do was wait."

Annie gathered her arms into her hands as if a gust of cold wind had hit her. Her face went white. "You mean we're too late?"

Uncle Otis reached to draw her into the living room, but her feet didn't move. "It was just about the time you started, I guess. Nobody expected —" He let his hand drop. "— it to happen," he said.

A moth rushed from the darkness and flung itself at the porch light. I've missed my grandfather, Stowe thought. He's dead.

He touched Annie's arm. "No," she said dimly. She turned toward the steps, her eyes darting without seeing. "I'll walk a few minutes," she said.

Stowe watched in horror as she disappeared into the night. He made a startled jerk as Aunt Fritzi's hand closed over his arm and drew him inside.

The room swallowed him up. The drawn curtains and heavy furniture seemed to press his skin. He had never seen little rugs laid over the main rug at all the places where heavy traffic might wear it out. He lifted his feet anxiously, trying to keep them from bolting for the door and racing after Annie.

Aunt Fritzi wiped her eyes with a pink tissue. "Oh, I knew it was going to be a terrible shock. It's always such a terrible shock. Even when you're expecting it."

But we weren't expecting it, Stowe explained inside. We laughed and talked. We stopped the train. And all the time he was dead and we didn't even feel it. The wonder of it stunned him.

Aunt Fritzi led him through halls to a kitchen. A middle-aged man was eating a wedge of pie. "Stowe, this is our boy, Harold," Aunt Fritzi said. The man got up still chewing and took Stowe's hand. She said, "That makes you two first cousins once removed."

The man put his hand on Stowe's shoulder. They looked into each other's eyes, and Stowe could see that no one else knew about the phone call they had shared.

"I'm sorry," Harold said. Stowe nodded, making a wordless sound. Harold sat down again and put another piece of pie on a clean saucer. "Have some," he said.

Stowe shook his head uncertainly. "I guess not. Thank you." Suddenly he was ravenous. He wasn't sure what emotion beyond shock he had expected to feel, but certainly not enthusiastic hunger. Slowly he sat and ate. It was peach pie, the best he had ever tasted.

Harold watched him. "Long trip," he said kindly when Stowe had finished.

"Yes."

Harold stood up. "Well, this first cousin's got to remove himself back home. Tell Annie I'll see her in the morning." He laid his saucer in the sink and went out the back door.

"He lives down by the shop," Uncle Otis said. He and Aunt Fritzi stood awkwardly beside the table, like strangers in their own kitchen. It was hard for them to know what to say, Stowe supposed. The strange silent war they had watched for thirteen years had ended, and they weren't sure who had won.

He said, "Your pie's good."

Aunt Fritzi made a little fidget of pleasure.

"Junior high?" Uncle Otis asked.

"I'll be in eighth grade," Stowe said, listening for Annie's footsteps on the porch.

Aunt Fritzi said, "I know you're tired after all that driving. Let me show you where you'll sleep. Otis, sweetheart, get their suitcases."

"I can," Stowe said, hoping to escape into the darkness as Annie had. But his great-uncle was already going out the door.

Aunt Fritzi led him through more halls to a little shed-roofed room. An old air-conditioner grumbled in one window, sending a drift of cool air out to battle the oven heat.

"I'm sorry I've still got these boxes and things stored in here," she said. "Your grandfather —" She paused, having the same trouble with the word he did. "Your grandfather asked me to clear out his house. Close it up. He didn't want such a big place to take care of. We said, Come stay with us, but he hadn't decided if he would or not, when . . ." She patted her pocket for more tissues, but she had used them up. "So we have all his things stored here."

Slowly Stowe looked around for clues to the man he had missed. One open-topped box had clothes in it. Grey coveralls. The tops of worn cowboy boots. Someone had written ANNIS across a tied-up box. And on a table, not yet boxed, were piles of books. With a start, he recognized a title he had heard before. *Of Mice and Men*. Tell me about the little house, George.

He felt a giant wave of homesickness rise and curl over him. He gulped a breath that would last until the wave broke and ebbed away. He was lost. His mountains had sunk into the earth and the world was flat.

Uncle Otis came in, holding out two cases. "The little one," Stowe whispered through the ache in his throat.

Aunt Fritzi patted his arm, and they left. He sat in the draft of cool air that smelled like mildew instead of pines.

Then Annie came, and sat beside him, and they held hands.

"It's all right," she said. Her face was crumpled from crying. "I needed a little time to get used to things. I hated to leave you, but I knew they'd want to talk, and explain, and — I just couldn't, yet."

"Can you now?" he asked.

"If I ever can." She got up and stroked the piles of books with shaky fingers, greeting them.

"He closed up his house," Stowe said. "Everything's here."

"Maybe he knew," Annie said. "Had a premonition. No. He didn't know. He couldn't have believed he was dying, and not ask for me." She pressed her forehead. "Are you tired?"

"Of this part."

She nodded, and tapped one of the books. "Dear old Robert Louis Stevenson. He was right, wasn't he? To travel hopefully was better than to arrive, this day. I don't think he meant it that way. But maybe he did. He never found health in all his searching, and died young, and left us *Treasure Island*."

"I wish we were home," Stowe said.

"I know." She went to the mirror hanging on the wall, and combed her hair with her fingers. "But this is hard for them, too. They're waiting to talk. We've got years of things to put to rest." Suddenly she braced her hands on either side of the mirror, and leaned her forehead against it, and both her faces shattered into tears.

# ❧ Seven ❧

"If you want to change any of the arrangements, Annis," Aunt Fritzi said at breakfast, "of course—"

Annie shook her head.

"We just went ahead yesterday," Aunt Fritzi said uneasily.

"Under the circumstances," Uncle Otis said.

"Of course," Annie said. "You knew what his wishes would have been."

In the middle of a bite, Stowe thought, The checks won't come anymore. His throat refused to swallow his biscuit and jam. How could he have thought of that, on this day?

At midmorning Harold came back in a dark suit, bringing his wife, Darlene. She put her arms around Stowe with casseroles in both hands. The kitchen began to fill with food from neighbors and friends.

A welter of people he couldn't keep straight took Stowe's hand and peered into his face. When he finally escaped to his room, he found a navy blue jacket and matching trousers draped over the foot of his bed.

Annie came in behind him. "No," he said. "I'm not wearing that stuff. I've got my own jeans and a T-shirt."

She held out the jacket until he tried it on.

"No!" he insisted, retracting his wrist bones to make the sleeves long enough.

"Yes," she said evenly. "Some things you just *do*. I don't like funerals, either, but it's a formality we have to get through, and it means something to them. Aunt Fritzi wanted this bad enough to borrow from a neighbor. So you'll wear it."

He jerked it off. Brownie would simply have flexed his shoulders and popped a seam, and that would have settled that. But he wasn't Brownie. He didn't have the shoulders for popping the seams of a borrowed coat. People had their own shapes.

It suddenly struck him that he was more upset over some kid's suit than he was his grandfather. The unreality of everything that was happening congealed into a heavy dread.

At two o'clock he put on the suit. They got into Uncle Otis's car and drove to the funeral home. An overcast sky pressed heat down on them. "We're suffering for a rain," Uncle Otis said, leaning to glare up at the dark clouds as he drove. "Driest summer in nine years — I hope this don't pass us up."

Behind him in the back seat, Aunt Fritzi said to Annie, "You understand how hard it was, being torn two ways so long. How can we make it up to you, sweetheart? Move back to Maydell. Otis and I want you to stay with us. We've got all that extra room, and the bookkeeping job at the shop is yours for the asking."

Stowe applied imaginary brakes, straining to hear what Annie would answer. But at the exact moment she spoke, Uncle Otis said, "So that old pickup of Chris's didn't give you any trouble. I sure didn't expect you to drive up in that thing."

"It did fine," Stowe said, turning worriedly to look at Annie. She smiled at him.

"Annis," Uncle Otis said, speaking to her face in the rearview mirror, "Harold would probably buy that old kettle off of you if you stay. He's going to need a pickup out there if he buys up any more hogs."

Annie smiled at Stowe. He made a jerk of disbelief. Why wasn't she saying, Hey, save your breath, we're not giving Horseless away to haul pigs in.

"Buy a little compact to get around town in," Uncle Otis told the mirror. "In a couple of years Stowe can get himself a motorcycle. And you're all set."

Stowe looked back at Annie. Motorcycle. That was an arrangement he hadn't thought of. She was still smiling but she looked like someone cornered, with her back to a wall.

They were directed through a chapel filled with strangers, to the front where empty seats were waiting. A bank of flowers almost hid a silvery casket covered with a little rug of carnations. Stowe glanced at Annie, puzzled. Was it possible that he wasn't going to have that first and last confrontation he had braced himself for? The unreality grew, numbing him.

Organ music came whining out from behind a grille, and disembodied voices sang a hymn. A solemn bean-pole man gave a talk about Lee Earl Albright, and forgot to say that he had a grandson he had never seen.

All the heads bent in a prayer. Stowe watched Annie's thumb gently rub the pricked tip of her middle finger. Obscenity, he thought. He would have to go through this nightmare two more times. With her, someday, And far ahead, almost into infinity, he would be the guest of honor at another artificial gathering like this, unless he could arrange to be lost at sea or blown to bits at the final moment.

Maybe even another time, he realized. If his father died, was he supposed to go to the funeral? Maybe people didn't, when they had sort of given up on each other. Would his father come to his?

He tried to think what he would feel if he looked down into the coffin and saw his father's dimly remembered face. For the first time ever, he took a long steady objective look. He saw a handsome man asleep who couldn't any longer hide things. He simply lay there, exposing how he'd been molded by his longings and the way his childhood went and all the other blundered-through experiences of his life.

Annie nudged him. The rug of carnations was gone. Someone had lifted half the casket's lid, and people were passing and peering with respectful curiosity.

The organ rolled. Stowe stared in amazement as Uncle Otis broke into a grin. Then he realized the sound had been thunder.

They moved closer, over carpet that gave under his feet like the pine-needle duff of old forests. He felt Annie's damp hand clamped over his. He tried to say through their twined fingers, It's like in the mountains — the trees turn into soil to feed the next trees, and it's all one thing.

Ahead of him, Uncle Otis stood a moment, sadly looking down. Stowe clamped off a sudden conglomerate of feelings, trying not to think of hell, and his exposed wrists, and Dracula.

Aunt Fritzi stepped closer, into the circle of Uncle Otis's arm, pressing her shredded pink tissue to her mouth. Stowe was near enough to see the inside edge of the casket. It had more satin and ruffles than Annie had ever put on the fanciest crib quilt. It didn't seem appropriate for a welder who liked cowboy boots. But it was Aunt Fritzi's way, he guessed, of showing, through the borrowed suit and the music and flowers, that she expected prettier things for him now. Stowe felt a little gust of kinship with the man who lay there out of sight.

Aunt Fritzi bent down to Stowe, gently smiling, her eyes puffy with grief. "Oh, doesn't he look natural?"

Stowe took a step forward and looked in at a big-nosed face with a carved mouth and scraggly grey eyebrows. All his mind could grasp was that his grandfather looked uncomfortable lying there on a satin pillow in his best suit and tie.

"Yes," he nodded, not wanting to remind her he had no way of knowing. He stood beside Annie, wondering if she was going to do something dramatic like in the movies. Throw herself on the casket, crying out Why? until someone led her away. But she only walked past slowly, letting her hand slide for a moment on the casket's steely edge, the way she had stroked Horseless the night the mirror fell and she had said acceptingly, *Never look back. Right?*

Rain was falling when they went outside, and the street sent up the good smell of hot wet concrete. A long string of cars followed the hearse to the cemetery. Stowe had been shifted into Harold's truck beside Darlene. She gave his knee a kind pat and said, "This must be really tough for you. Especially your mother." She waited, but he couldn't guess what she wanted him to reveal. "She can't help but be bitter. I watched all this foolishness from the sidelines, you know. I'd have to hate anybody as mule-headed as her dad." She looked around. "Good Lord forgive me for saying that, but it can't hurt him now."

"She didn't hate him," Stowe said. "She wanted to come. To make up." He stared through the windshield wipers' sweeps. In the silence of his mind he said, I hated him, though. I didn't give her the chance to come.

Darlene sighed. "Well, I truly believe he's in a better place and knows you were trying to forgive and forget."

Stowe squirmed, to shift the heaviness that was cutting off his breath. What if his grandfather *was* in some new place, all wise and different, and could look into people's hearts?

"I don't suppose it would be appropriate, under the circumstances, to let your daddy know," Darlene said.

He watched the rain runnels twisting on the windows. He figured Annie still had the address in her purse, for emergencies. This must not have been an emergency. "I don't guess so." He wished he could go numb, and not have to think or feel or respond to anything else. He didn't want to wonder if, somewhere out there, another man who hadn't gone to a better place was waiting for his forgiveness without any new wisdom or love.

"I feel really bad that I didn't beg you harder to come, when I called," Harold said. "It would've made so much difference. Even a day sooner."

The heaviness fell on him. "I know," he managed to say. He squeezed his eyes shut. Oh, God. Help me. What did I do? He could see the back of Annie's head in Uncle Otis's car in front of them. All those years, he had hated two men for giving her pain. And had never once thought, Will I?

They turned in at the cemetery. People skittered from their cars to the canopy. Wet flowers drooped on a bank of artificial grass around the grave. The pallbearers stood with their backs to the rain, trying not to look glad as it poured down. The casket rested on straps that would roll out. Stowe stared at it, thinking his grandfather would have understood that mechanical part better than the rest, and would have taken pleasure in seeing it work properly. But no one was allowed to see it work. After a final prayer, the little group hurried back to the cars. The women covered their hair with their purses, and only Annie looked up at the sky.

Stowe squeezed in beside her. She was wet with rain, but she smiled and indicated the old trees and tombstones. "It's pretty here."

How can you do that? he asked her. How long are you going to smile at me?

He looked back as they pulled away. The casket was gone. Something in him dropped away, too — gone, final, heavy. He almost flung out his hands to brace his fall. He wanted to grab at something, the way little kids did when they were being hauled along, so he wouldn't have to

171

think like an adult, or understand things, or ever die.

I could have liked him, he thought. We could have welded things. And now we can't ever. Oh, don't die, he said without words to everyone, to Annie beside him, to the traffic passing. What would I do, loving you like I do? It hurts too much.

He faced forward again. In a way, he wondered, were his father and grandfather the smart ones? Choosing not to risk that hurtfulness?

Late in the afternoon Harold rescued Stowe from the lava flow of unknown relatives and neighbors that crept through the living room. They went out to the shop and Harold showed him the big arc welder, and the cylinders of acetylene gas, and the heavy flatbed truck with portable welding equipment on it. "You know, Stowe, we'd teach you all about this business," Harold said. "If you and your mother moved here to Maydell. Make a welder out of you."

Stowe's stomach contracted. He didn't know how to answer. A part of him would have reached out eagerly to put on a black helmet and take hold of a hissing torch. But the main part held back, not sure how Annie felt about the sudden invitation to change their lives, or how he felt himself.

He tried to find a time to ask her, but people visited, and when he finally caught her alone in the kitchen that evening, she was writing thank-you notes for the flowers and food that people had sent.

"Why can't Aunt Fritzi do that?" he asked.

"People sent some of these things to say they're sorry for how things were, and to welcome us back."

He sat and watched her, occasionally lifting a pecan from the top of a cake. He wondered what Brownie was doing. Dodging the law? Weeks seemed to have gone by since they ate pork chops peacefully, friends again.

Annie put her pen down and hunched across the table. "Let's sneak off," she whispered.

They eased silently out the back door. The rain had stopped and little frogs were celebrating the end of the drought. They crossed the vacant lot through wet weeds, and gazed at the dark closed house where Annie had grown up.

"That was my window," she said, pointing. "I had the sunrises."

And the comic opera, yes-oh-thank-you night, he thought, when she was rescued.

They walked on. "Aunt Fritzi said my dad made a will a year or so ago. Uncle Otis and Harold will keep the shop. Aunt Fritzi gets the personal things. And the house—" She let out her breath in a laugh and drew it sadly in again. "The money from the house goes to an organization for homeless boys. I think that's what is known as the final irony."

Stowe looked back at the house. "You would've liked to have it."

She thought about it. "In a way. Yes. The security of it. Especially for you. To feel permanent. Rooted. To be able to keep your childhood longer. But on the other hand . . ." She carefully walked a curb to miss a puddle.

"It's already decided. So in a way it's a relief not to have to make a choice."

He understood. He felt the same way about the man he would never have to face and forgive, or not forgive.

"They want us to move here," he said. "Even without the house. They say they've got room for us in their house."

"They have," Annie said, with no emotion he could catch. "It's a big old solid house. It might be what we need, Stowe. They've offered me a job. It's been difficult for them and they feel free to accept us now."

"They never had to feel the way he felt. Didn't they have minds of their own?"

She shrugged. "Loyalty's a complicated thing. But they're trying hard to make it up to us. We'd be surrounded by kind people in that house."

His stomach got the seasick wobbles again. "But it wouldn't be ours."

The bushes twanged with insects that fell silent as they passed. "No, it wouldn't. But, Stowe, neither is the house we rent." She paused, regretful. "And you know, don't you, that the house we talk about at Sutherland's Camp isn't ever going to be ours, either. It's a dream. There's no way we can have it."

He felt lightning-struck. He batted the sparkles of shock out of his eyes. "You can't say what I'm going to have!" he said, amazed at her. "Or what I'm going to be. Or anything! It's got to be left open. And staying here wouldn't leave it open. It'd be like saying we don't believe." He willed a picture into his mind. The letter in the mailbox, waiting right this minute at home. Congratulations! How could she say he had to let go of all his grand plans for taking care of her? He would never never turn loose of them, except to get a better grip "It'd be like saying we're scared."

"Aren't we scared?" Annie asked.

"No!" he shouted. "Where's the rising ground here in this place? Where's the climbing to reach the top?"

She stopped in the middle of the road. Far to the east, the storm front shivered with sheet lightning. "I think we'd better turn back," she said.

"I don't *want* their too-late guilty-feeling jobs and houses and pats on the head," he said loudly.

She walked past him as if she hadn't heard.

Aunt Fritzi was bending over a box in his room when he started in.

"Oh, don't mind me," she puffed. "I'm just finding this for your mother."

Annie appeared at the door, looking pale.

Aunt Fritzi lifted a box from the floor and opened it on the table. She looked in, doubt and nervousness puckering her face, and said, "I didn't know what to do, Annis. I didn't want to upset you, but it was so personal I knew I had to tell you about it."

Annie looked into the box. Her mouth twitched.

"What?" Stowe asked.

Annie lifted out a small packet of envelopes held together by a rubber band. Gently she riffled it.

"What?" Stowe asked.

Aunt Fritzi gave Annie a glance. Annie said, "Your grandfather saved the letters I sent him every month. Little bundles. Twelve in each."

175

"Thirteen years of bundles," Aunt Fritzi said. "I found them when I cleared out his desk and I just couldn't — " She made a hesitant throwing-away gesture. "When he'd saved them."

Annie said, "I'm glad you showed me. I wouldn't have known." She stroked them, and put them back. "I wondered, sometimes, if he just threw them away unopened. This makes me feel — " She reached for a word to describe her emotion, and let her hand fall, because there was no word.

Somewhere, in there, Stowe thought, was the last thing she ever said to him. What was she thinking? About the days of talking they might have had, if he had let her come in time?

Annie said, "I regret how much I must have hurt him, every letter, talking about Stowe, telling what a joy *my* son was, how big, how full of life, when *his* son was dead. I didn't think."

Stowe stared out the window at the darkness. Horseless, slumped patiently out there in the driveway, was the only thing belonging to his uncle Chris that he would ever have the chance to touch or love.

"They looked so neat," Aunt Fritzi said apologetically, "I thought you might like to put them away, and someday Stowe could read them. They would be almost like a monthly journal of his childhood."

Annie smiled. "He might like that." She gave him a questioning glance. Slowly he smiled back.

"And, Annis," Aunt Fritzi said, "if you'd like any of these things — I feel so uncomfortable about that part of his will. Since they're all mine now, you know all you have to do is ask. The books, the clothes? Furniture?"

Annie looked at Stowe. He got his pajamas out of his suitcase. "I would like the books," he said.

He watched surprise widen Annie's eyes and slowly soften to gratitude. He wondered where she had sat in that dark house across the vacant lot, reading her dad's old books while she waited for Mr. Culture.

"Stowe," Aunt Fritzi said, "help me talk your mother into staying here. This ought to be home. We just can't let you go back up there to a rented house when we've got all this space."

They looked at her, and then at each other.

"And a job at the shop, just like old times," Annie said, pressing her lips tight.

Aunt Fritzi brightened. "Oh, old times reminds me. Annis, one of your old flames moved back to Maydell after his divorce. You remember Jimmy Wicks."

"No," Annie said. Stowe turned, on his way to the bathroom with his pajamas. He waited.

"Oh, you do," Aunt Fritzi insisted. She giggled. "He keeps asking about you. He runs the motel. And handsomer than ever."

"That's nice," Annie said. "He shouldn't have any trouble attracting somebody who remembers him."

"Now, Annis, don't be flip. I'm just concerned. It's obvious you're just barely managing. Just getting by, sweetheart. You're not going to make it on your own."

Stowe saw defensiveness and then sarcasm flick across her face. She smiled. "You mean all this mothering and homemaking and sharing interests and being emotionally secure doesn't count, and what we really need is a man to pay the bills and run our lives properly?"

"I just know the statistics," Aunt Fritzi said tartly. "Husbands help."

Annie spread her hands. "Aunt Fritzi, I've got to do it my way. I've got to think—"

"Well, you've got to do it Stowe's way, too, Annis, and think what you owe him. He's not a baby anymore. You can't build your life around him and use him to make up for all your failures."

Stowe froze in the doorway. As he watched, pain slowly reshaped Annie's face. It scared him. Was it possible that she could take a job she hated and live in somebody else's house and give up her mountains and her dreams, for him?

Would he, for her?

Suddenly Annie turned toward him with such intensity that he jumped. "Am I doing that?" She looked at him with a soft scared version of his grandfather's face.

He stared back, feeling wintery shivers start inside. He said, "It's all right, if you are. I—I know you use me. I know I'm the most important thing in your life. It's kind of like a burden to me, sure." A hot rush of self-forgetfulness stopped the shivers. "But I was a burden to you, and you turned it into something else. Like you said. A joy."

Annie sat down on his bed, with the pack of letters in her lap. "You're still a joy," she said. "I love you more than anything in the world. You're all I have. So I'm one of those possessive mothers." She flicked a smile at Aunt Fritzi's unyielding face.

"I didn't say that," Aunt Fritzi said.

"Maybe the way we love each other seems too close for some tastes." Annie turned her smile on him. "Even yours, Stowe. But spaces will come between us. You'll change into a father and a middle-aged man, and we'll love each other in a different way." She smoothed the letters. "I love you in a different way already than when you were a little helpless child, don't I?"

"Yes," he said in a wobbly voice.

"And there'll be other people in my life. Even a husband, Aunt Fritzi, if it happens that way. Or a daughter-in-law and grandchildren. And always my passing-through children — babies over and over. And, Stowe, all the love ahead for you! Your family and work and friends — " A tear dropped into her lap. She blotted it off a letter. "Don't ever tack it to the wall. Spend it, Stowe. Keep it moving, pass it through as many hands as you possibly can." She held the letters out to him. "Don't let this happen."

He stood frozen in remorse. "Oh, jeez, don't," he begged. "I'm sorry! I didn't know we'd be too late. I should've told you, the minute he called." Rocks dammed up his throat until only a trickle of words could come. "I just didn't want to. I knew, when I did, it wouldn't be just us-against-the-world anymore. Against him anymore. Like it always was. When it was so much fun. Being alike."

"Called?" Aunt Fritzi said, puzzled.

He said, "I thought if you could just ignore him, like I do my—" He swerved from that direction. "And not let him matter. But he did. And I didn't give you a chance to tell him or show him—"

Annie stood up, and the letters fell. She came and put her arms around him. He let her, with Aunt Fritzi right there staring. He bit his lips tight to keep his face from dissolving all away. "Stowe," she said. "It wasn't you. I could have called. I could have asked questions, and pawned things, and *come*. But I was waiting to be asked for. With a guaranteed welcome. I was too proud—he had to say he wanted me. I couldn't say it first."

She held him hard. The way he had clutched the just-us feeling that had held his life together and kept him safe and made him strong.

Aunt Fritzi picked up the letters. "Oh, Annis," she murmured. "Sweetheart. Stowe. You know you have a guaranteed welcome."

Annie turned him loose, and smiled. "I know we do. Thank you." She looked into Stowe's eyes.

He braced himself. He knew all he had to do was say what he wanted, and it would be. But he didn't want what *he* wanted. It was scary to realize, but somebody else's happiness mattered more than his.

"You choose," he said.

She turned back to Aunt Fritzi. "You've offered us something really special." Stowe took a silent, preparing breath. "But we like what we have, Aunt Fritzi."

He felt like a taut balloon someone had just let go. He shot up with a blast of hope.

"You can't live hand-to-mouth like that," Aunt Fritzi said reasonably. "You've got to be practical."

"No," Annie said. "We've got to be in accord. And we've got to go home."

Stowe threw his pajamas straight up in the air.

"But, Annis, it isn't reasonable — "

"No. But my children are waiting."

"And my friend's taking my paper route," Stowe said. He pulled his pajama top down from the light fixture where it had caught. He had never felt so good.

They left in the early, Sunday-morning stillness, with little plastic containers of funeral food in the picnic box. Horseless hummed.

The letters and the cartons of books rode in the back, under a tarp Uncle Otis had given them. Harold had come by as they were leaving, and had given Stowe a crowbar half as tall as he was. Harold said, "Next time you come, you can take back some more of those old tools you admired out there in the shop." Stowe's throat had closed up with affection as he nodded.

They climbed slowly out of the shallow river valley where Maydell huddled, and started off across the plains. The trees had disappeared and every mile of horizon was empty against the sky when Annie said, out to the road ahead, "I'm not a daughter anymore."

Stowe nodded. He gave her a quick glance, to see if she looked different.

She batted the bewilderment out of her eyes, and sat up straight and passed a cattle truck. Stowe grinned, helping

Horseless by pushing on the dash. Annie said, "Child, thanks for bearing with me, and helping me get to this point finally. I know it wasn't easy."

He said, "You and Horseless have horsepower you haven't even used yet."

"I hope," she said, and smiled. They watched the tiny changes in the land. A patch of sunflowers faced east. A little crack of erosion took off across a hill like a river system on a map. "I dreamed about my dad last night. I dreamed he left us the house. And then, when I woke up, I decided he had been wise, not to. Maybe he was telling us we had all we needed, already."

"Maybe so," Stowe said, marveling that a tiny twist of thought might have kept them from settling down inside that empty shell, with all its ghosts.

"I lay there thinking, maybe he held off loving us so we could grow tough and determined."

That had never occurred to him. "You mean, like as long as he never gave in, then we wouldn't either?" It almost made sense that he would hold out against them so they could hold out against the world.

He thought of something himself, that he wasn't sure he could explain.

"Maybe he really loved you all the time," he said with care. "A lot. Maybe more than he thought he should. So he sort of tried to stop being so close, and got pals with your brother, and then when you wanted to leave and get married it hurt him so much he just filled up his mind with things like you chose a worthless man and all."

She drove in silence a long time. He knew by the whiteness of her knuckles on the steering wheel that she wanted to ask, What made you think that? Us? And he also knew that loving was too complicated and individual for any kind of answer, and she wouldn't ask.

They went through a little town, slowing at a cross-walk for people walking toward a church. Through the trees they could see a rose window of stained glass.

"Why didn't I just go back years ago and force him to let me into his life?" Annie asked. "Oh, Stowe, I regret that."

"Why? You tried," he said. Maybe not enough. But seeing it now didn't help. "You wrote him. You didn't give up on him. I'm the one that didn't try. I didn't even bother to feel anything. Or even back you up, or offer to go visit, or anything."

They passed a second church, smaller, surrounded by weeds on the edge of town. A bell suddenly clanged in its stubby little tower.

He drew a long turning-loose breath. "I don't want to feel that way about my father." He looked out, afraid to watch her face. "I don't want him and me to repeat what you and your dad did."

After a long time she said, "You mean, like what if he died." Stowe nodded. He knew he had just crossed a point in his life, just as quickly and finally as Horseless crossed a bridge. He was in different country. He couldn't go on resenting his father and risk watching him become Lee Earl Albright all over again, bitter and lonely and cheated of part of his life.

"I know you keep his address," he said.

"Yes."

He waited. His mouth went dry. He was asking for something that would complicate his life. It could mean pain and rejection and scary newness. He watched Horseless's shadow on the railroad embankment as it stretched and bulged over the changing slope. We'll have to change like that, he thought. Stretch and shrink to fit what comes.

"In my purse," Annie said. "Behind my driver's license."

He opened the worn clasp and took out a folded paper. Without opening it he slid it into his shirt pocket.

When he saw her tears he said, "This doesn't mean I'll use it. Maybe not for a while. But when I'm ready."

"I know," she said. "I understand." She wiped her nose. "It's just that you've always been here. Built into my life. Coo," she said softly, "it was beautiful when you belonged just to me."

For a moment he felt the same quivering regret that he heard in her voice. He wanted to say, It's because you gave me so much love that I've got it left over for him. And for your dad, and myself, and the world.

"Hey," he said. "I'm still here. I just might write him, is all. And see what happens." He hoped she understood he was saying it was all right, she could still lean on him while they both grew stronger. His time would come, the way hers had.

"I know," she said. "It's all right. But I've got to warn you. I'm going to stay a part of your life." She shot him one of her steady, anxious glances.

"Sure," he said easily.

"I'll try not to be too meddlesome, but I'm going to be there. So brace yourself. We belong to each other."

He let his face droop in pretend dismay. "You mean I've got to keep on doing what's right, and wondering how

184

you'd like for me to act, and stuff like that, the rest of my life?"

Suddenly she laughed. "No. Just the rest of *my* life. Then you're on your own."

He pretended to shrug in resignation. "By that time I'll probably be so used to it, I'll go on doing it anyway."

Annie nodded, smiling. "That's the whole idea, child."

Horseless grumbled to a stop. Stowe sat up alertly, trying to pretend his long nap had been just a second's rest for his eyes. Annie had pulled into the same road where they had eaten lunch before. She kept on driving until they eased over a little gravelly rise and the railroad tracks disappeared.

"We don't want to utterly confuse that poor train crew, in case they happen by," she said, turning Horseless around in a wide spot.

They put down the tailgate and set Aunt Fritzi's little plastic containers out. With plastic spoons they filled the paper plates she had sent, making heaping mixtures of casseroles and salads and vegetables. Stowe thought of how many friends and neighbors those piles of food represented. People who had liked his grandfather, or his mother. Or both. They stuffed themselves.

"Now back to my cooking," Annie said wistfully, licking a plastic lid.

Stowe sighed. "Even worse than that. Back to school." He had just realized it, staring at the end-of-summer yellow in the weeds. Back to school where the clocks ran slower than the summer-clocks of home.

"Life goes on," Annie said. "And on. And on."

He nodded. It had been a summer of goodbyes. He said, "I was thinking. We could tell Sir Landlard we'd paint the house for a month's rent."

Annie's face lit up. "The idea of a genius." She pulled her back straight. "And in the meantime I'll see about adding a couple more kids."

He sighed, but nodded again, thinking that after lawn-mowing season would come selling Saturday papers at football games, then snow-shoveling. Then another summer, with real jobs.

"Maybe some co-op place will take crib quilts and stuffed toys," Annie said.

And there were the letters, he thought. The letters that were absolutely coming, because he would never stop asking until he was answered. Dear sir. Congratulations. You have just won your own fantastic dream house, to be built at the site of your choice. You have just won. You have.

They walked along the road, rolling their stiff necks. Annie said, "There's a marvelous made-up word in a book called *Finnegans Wake*. Gracehopers."

"Grasshoppers?" he asked, hearing the whirring in the weeds.

"No. Gracehopers. We're gracehopers."

He said, "I guess we are," storing it with the things she was always saying that he didn't understand. They turned back toward Horseless waiting in the heat. "I'm going to take automobile mechanics in school," he said.

She nodded, looking glad.

"I'll learn to fix everything that goes wrong," he said. "I'll keep this old piece of junk running like silk."

They leaned on Horseless's grille. Annie wiped one dusty headlight with the tail of her shirt. Stowe wiped the other. She wrote WASH ME across the hood with her finger, and looked around. "It's a nice, quiet, unused road," she said.

Stowe took a long surrendering breath. "Can I drive?"

She handed him the keys. "Stop before you strand Horseless on the tracks. That would *really* stop their train."

He expected her to get in and sit in his place, but she only smiled and walked on down the road in the direction he would go.

He got in, feeling nauseous with excitement. He could drive, he kept reminding himself. He had started Horseless dozens of times. He had watched Annie for years. He fumbled the key into the switch, and turned it. One foot pressed the brake and the other nudged the starter. The roar of the engine tingled his scalp. He eased his foot off the brake. Horseless quivered like a Thoroughbred waiting for the command to go. Stowe wet his lips. Annie sauntered on, not looking back.

He shifted into gear. Horseless bucked and started off. He was moving. He was driving. Weeds were going past. The wheel, hot and firm, was relaying his orders to Horseless as he steered.

He honked. Annie spun around, beaming, and watched him come.

Suddenly she did the little shuffle in the road that they had done after they stopped the train. Her hand flicked a greeting as he passed, laughing. Not a hint of needing help. Just a wave that didn't ask for anything but a waggle of fingers in return.

He drove on until he could see the railroad tracks. Grandly, perfectly, he braked to a stop and turned the engine off. He could hear the slap of her sandals as she ran to catch up. He opened the door for her, and slid from the driver's seat into his own.